A CHANCE OF

SNOW

A Chance of

Carol Andersen

TATE PUBLISHING
AND ENTERPRISES, LLC

Published by Tate Publishing & Enterprises, LLC
127 E. Trade Center Terrace | Mustang, Oklahoma 73064 USA
1.888.361.9473 | www.tatepublishing.com

Tate Publishing is committed to excellence in the publishing industry. The company reflects the philosophy established by the founders, based on Psalm 68:11,
"The Lord gave the word and great was the company of those who published it."

Book design copyright © 2013 by Tate Publishing, LLC. All rights reserved.
Cover design by Lauro Talibong
Interior design by Jake Muelle

Published in the United States of America

ISBN: 978-1-62510-523-3
1. Fiction / General
2. Fiction / Contemporary Women
13.01.17

Dedication

To Pat Cunning for her sharp insight and encouragement, to Craig for his painstaking editing, constructive criticism, and sense of design, to Bob Paquet for a solid critical read, to Fran Preston for the research, and all the Vermont "stuff," to Katie, Jess, and Steph, my granddaughters, for their deliciously wicked imaginations, and to Orrin for giving me the time and space to get the job done.

Carol Andersen
march 2014

PROLOGUE

The air around the bar was heavy with the odors of greasy food and stale cigarette smoke. Stifling afternoon heat had emptied the place except for Carly, who was still on the deck, and a couple of regulars slouched on stools inside, chain-smoking and slugging back cold beers from dripping plastic mugs. In a sun-bleached bikini, she half-reclined on the splintery deck chair, her long tanned legs forming a shady bridge over the dog at her feet. Damp auburn curls clung to her neck and forehead. Sweat rolled along her throat and settled between her breasts.

It was after five o'clock, and the hours of scorching sun and multiple margaritas were finally delivering their mind-numbing stupor, pinning her to the wooden chair like a blanket of bricks. She struggled to keep her eyes open, afraid to let the nightmare images creep inside her brain again.

Needing distraction, she straightened up in the chair and watched the last of the beach stragglers pack up their screaming kids, empty coolers, and umbrellas and head for their cars, stepping gingerly on the hot pavement in the parking lot. Dozens of sandpipers dodged small waves as they scrambled frantically back and forth along the shoreline, poking about in the wet sand for their supper. The searing sun had begun to lower, burning the remains of the late winter day blood red before it dropped into the horizon. A ship's horn sounded at the harbor entrance as a rusty shrimp boat entered the narrows, escorted by an entourage of hungry mewling gulls. Carly raised her soggy paper cup in a weak salute to the captain of the *Annie Rose* as it chugged by the fish shanty pier. The captain signaled a return greeting with the cockpit bell, and she laid back in the deck chair again, soothed by the soft steady lapping of the boat's wake against the pilings. Random puffs of warm air teased but did not cool her.

Walking up behind her, the bartender let his eyes feast on the supple curves of her body before breaking into her silence.

"Ready for another, Carly?"

The dog looked up, startled by the intrusion, and then took a protective position in the front of Carly's chair. She looked at the bartender, wide-eyed with surprise.

"Oh my god, Danny, don't do that. You scared me! You even scared Silk. Thanks anyway. I'm all set for now. And don't creep up on me like that again!"

She settled back once again, desperately trying to recapture her torpid state, but the sounds of the lapping waves and the feel of the soft breezes gave way to visions of driving snow, scraping metal, blood, sirens, police, and the horrendous accident that changed the course of her life. Her throat tightened as she tried to hold back the sob rising in her throat, and she shut her eyes, trying to contain the spill of tears.

In the distance, a man was walking along the shoreline, wading in and out of the warm water as he moved forward. He picked a careful path across the rough stone jetties as he made his way toward the fish shanty. Silk saw him first and sat up quickly, watching intently as the man got closer to the pier. Carly stood up to see what had caught the dog's attention. Shading her eyes with her hand, she could see the heat-rippled figure walking along the water's edge, but she couldn't tell who it was. The dog knew, and he scrambled down the rickety wooden steps of the deck and onto the hot sand, barking happily as he ran to meet the approaching figure.

The snow doesn't give a soft white damn whom it touches.

—e.e.cummings

All changes, even the most longed for, have their melancholy; for what we leave behind us is a part of ourselves; we must die to one life before we can enter another.

—Anatole France

ONE

The day started out gray and damp, with a gusty northeast wind and a promise of snow, typical weather for Boston in early March. It was only eleven o'clock in the morning, but the dark skies made it seem like late afternoon. Carly's third-floor office had a panoramic view of Boston Harbor, and she watched the shallow waters being whipped into a white-capped froth by the approaching storm. Nets of sea spray were flung against the windows by the gusty northeast winds and the few boats docked in the marina rocked wildly against the wooden pilings and piers. She shivered slightly and pulled her jacket tightly across her chest. Her desk was cluttered with stacks of client folders needing attention but she was unable to focus on them. It had been three months since her fiancé had been killed in a roadside accident, and his picture, smiling at her from its frame on the desk, reminded her of how much she missed him. Memories of that night constantly disrupted her thoughts and were especially vivid during stormy weather. She sat back in her desk chair as the images of the accident completely overtook her. She relived the events over and over again, the details as vivid as the day they happened.

She had been listening to storm reports all that day, and the forecasters had been predicting just a chance of snow, which, in Carly's mind, was nothing to be concerned about. Their wedding ceremony was in four days, and she was praying that Mother Nature would be cooperative and keep any serious snow at bay.

She was relieved that the day was finally over for her because her patience had been exhausted by the whining and complaining of the wealthy blue-haired old ladies and their CPAs who had met with her to review their trust funds and other holdings. It was days like these that made her wish that her father hadn't brought her into the firm.

Just as she was locking up, he appeared at her office door with an armful of manila folders. George Richardson was a handsome man with an imposing presence and an authoritative voice that he had learned to use to his advantage in and out of court.

"Carly, you're not leaving, I hope. It's only two thirty. I wanted to meet with you about Mrs. Holcomb's new will," he said.

"Dad, in case you forgot, tonight is our wedding rehearsal party! You *do* remember that Rob and I are being married in four days, don't you?"

"You don't need to be sarcastic with me, Charlotte," he snapped. "I did not forget that your wedding is in four days, but I don't recall that you told me you were leaving early today!"

"I'm sure I told you, Dad, but if I didn't, I'm sorry. I've had a lot to do this week."

His eyes narrowed as he looked at her with annoyance.

"Well, I guess it will just have to wait until Monday, won't it?" he said in his most sarcastic tone.

George Richardson was neither a forgiving nor a tolerant man, and he was clearly unhappy with his only child at the moment.

"I hope you didn't leave anything else unfinished because I haven't got time to clean up after you right now," he said as he turned and headed back to his office. "And don't forget that we have a meeting with David Oliver Monday afternoon. I expect you to be there on time!"

He marched off down the long corridor to his office, grumbling just loud enough for Carly to hear him. She started to say something to him but ended up going back into her own office, shaking her head in disbelief at her father's insensitivity.

"Tyrant!" she mumbled under her breath.

She finished locking her office and bundled herself up in a down coat and a warm pair of Wellies before she left the building and headed down Atlantic Avenue for the train station. Snow had already started to fall, and quarter-sized wet flakes were splattering the pavement, melting as they hit. It was still in the upper thirties, too mild, she thought, for the snow to stick to the ground and too mild to worry about traveling later that evening. When she got off at her station, she stopped to pick up Silk from the pet sitter on the way. He was a larger-than-average golden retriever, and she had been lucky to find someone who had the room to keep him during the day. He ran to the door as soon as he heard her coming up the steps, happy to be going home. They walked the few short blocks to the apartment, stopping at every hydrant and hedge so that Silk could leave his mark. Carly fed him as soon as they got home, and he settled into a corner of the overstuffed sofa with one of his favorite toys tucked under his chin.

Rob arrived around four o'clock, frosted with a dusting of snow on his clothing and in his black hair. Carly had fixed a plate of cheese and fruit, and they sat and relaxed for a while before changing their clothes. Rob had just been made a junior partner in one of Boston's most prestigious law firms, and it was not often that he managed to be home before eight o'clock at night. It was a luxury for them to just sit and relax, with a promise of dinner before nine o'clock. By five thirty, Carly announced that they needed to get moving.

Massachusetts Avenue was always a parking lot during afternoon rush hour, but the snow made it worse. What should have been a twenty-minute ride downtown took an hour, and Carly and Rob were the last to arrive at their own party. Henri, the maître d', was running around, wringing his hands, worried that the meal would spoil, and the party, along with his reputation, would be ruined. When the guests of honor finally arrived, a sigh of relief swept across the entire dining room. Henri pranced out of the kitchen, clapping his hands and shouting a welcome.

"Ah, ma chéri," he gushed at Carly. "I was so afraid that you would miss your party! Mon dieu! What a disaster we would have had. But come, come, you are here now. We can celebrate."

He kissed her on both cheeks, hugged Rob, and then fluttered away again into the kitchen to commandeer his staff into action. Carly stood wide-eyed at the entrance to the banquet room, amazed at the Winter Wonderland scene that Henri had orchestrated.

The party had been arranged by Rachel Ashe, Carly's best friend from their Phillips Exeter days, and Kevin Reid, Rob's college roommate. Henri was a good friend of the Reid family and helped keep the plans for the party relatively drama free. Henri, always a flamboyant chef and host, had outdone himself with the menu and the decorations.

The party was still going strong at ten o'clock when Henri appeared at the kitchen door, waving his arms frantically for Kevin and Rachel to go into the kitchen. He ushered them quickly through the swinging doors.

"Mes amis, we must end the party. I am so sorry, but I have been asked to close up now because the weather, it is very bad outside. The manager, he will not have any excuses. We must clean up now and leave, tout de suite," he said.

For a moment, they were silent with disappointment, but then they called Rob and Carly away from the dining room.

"Rob, Henri says we need to shut the party down. Looks like the weather has turned pretty nasty out there," Kevin said.

Carly stood at the double doors with Rachel while Henri, Kevin, and Rob left the dining area and moved out into the lobby where they headed for the elevator. Rob shot Carly an anxious look before he disappeared behind the elevator doors. She decided to follow them and sent Rachel back to the dining room to start breaking the news to the other guests.

The three men stood outside the revolving glass doors, huddled close to the building. Carly could barely move the door open because the wind, blowing from the northeast, was pounding the front of the building. She remained inside, watching the snow blowing sideways across the quiet street. Rob came back in first.

"Carly, this looks pretty bad. Whatever happened to 'a chance of snow?'" Rob said.

"I don't know, but Henri is right. This looks dangerous, and we need to get everyone going," Carly replied.

The four headed back to the function room, concerned now about the safety of their guests.

"Hey, everyone," Robert yelled to the group. "It's really bad out there. I think we need to get going, and if anyone doesn't feel fit to drive, let me know, and we'll find you another way home." Sighs of disappointment were followed by a slow exodus from the banquet room. Carly was worried and getting nervous about the drive home. She took Rob aside.

"Rob, do you think it's safe to drive?" she asked. "Maybe we should just stay at one of the hotels tonight."

"We can just take it slow. We'll be okay. Besides, we can't leave Silk all by himself overnight!"

"I could have one of the neighbors look in on him."

"No, we'll be okay. The Audi is good in the snow. Stop worrying and get your coat," he said.

The driving was hazardous, the worst Carly had seen in a long time. Wet snow had frozen on the pavement and had been covered by a few inches of lighter snow, making the roads icy and treacherous. Visibility was down to just a few feet, and the defroster in the car was unable to keep up with the snow piling up in the corners of the windshield. They heard on the radio that the DPW had been caught off guard by the quick turn of the storm and had not yet been out to treat the roads with salt or plows, making the going very slow and very slippery. The main roads were nearly empty of traffic, and as they inched their way toward Exit 26 for Storrow Drive, they noticed several cars off to the side of the road, all facing in different directions from having skidded on the slick surface. They should have been able to see the lights on the Zakim Bridge, but the snow was flying directly at them, giving them visibility for only a few feet ahead of them. Carly clenched the armrest with a white-knuckle grip. Rob was intense and rigid at the steering wheel, fearing that the car would go into a slide at any moment. Neither one spoke.

They were watching for the Storrow Drive exit sign to appear ahead of them when Rob suddenly lost control of the car. He tried to right it, but it spun around twice before coming to a hard stop in a snowdrift at the top of the exit ramp. They were stuck.

Rob tried shifting into forward and then reverse to free the vehicle, but it wouldn't budge from the rutted snow. "Carly, I have to get out and see if I can free up the front tires," he said. "I want you to stay in the car and shift it when I tell you. I have a shovel in the trunk and some Ice Melt, I think. That should get us moving."

She nodded and slid into the driver seat while Rob walked around to the rear of the car. By now there was no visibility at all, and she lost sight of him the minute he got out of the car. She pushed at the hazard light button, hoping that any oncoming vehicles would be able to see the flashing red lights. She heard the trunk slam shut with a thud and watched a spectral image of Rob pass by the driver side window and go to the front of the car.

She could hear him digging around the driver side wheel, but she couldn't see him. Snow continued to accumulate on the windshield, and the rear window was covered by snow so quickly that the defroster was not able to keep the glass clear. The only visibility Carly had was what she could see from the driver side window. She opened it and tried to call to Rob to see if he was all right, but the wind drowned her voice as it howled around the car.

TWO

B oston called all its snow removal equipment into emergency service on the night of December 27. The forecasters had totally missed the mark with their predictions of a chance of light snow, and the plows sat at the depots longer than they should have.

Plow 37 was driven by a new employee with very little experience. He had owned a construction company and had driven some heavy equipment, but never a snowplow of this size. He lied when he told the crew boss that he had driven large plows plenty of times. In fact, he had never driven a plow of this capacity, but he needed the work desperately and would have said anything to get the road job that night. He was nervous when he rolled the truck out onto the expressway and lowered his blade. His was one of the larger vehicles in service, a huge Mack truck with a wide-angled plow used for making half-road sweeps in one pass on the highways. He struggled with the gears a few times before getting the clutch into the right position. The truck made a few loud gasping sounds as it lurched forward into gear.

He entered Route 93 about a mile from the Storrow Drive exit. There were very few vehicles on the road, and visibility was near zero. He kept the headlights as low as he could, but the whiteout was severe, and he had to drive as close to the roadside as possible, just to keep a mark on his position. He heard the plow blade scraping against the pavement as he pushed the heavy snow aside. It was difficult for him to tell where he was because he could barely see the green-and-white overhead road signs until he was almost on top of them. For a moment, he thought he saw a glimmer of a flashing red light ahead of him, but it disappeared in a gust of wind-blown snow. He saw the red lights again, just before the blade of the plow hit something in its path. The sound of metal scraping metal was like fingernails running along a chalkboard. He knew he had hit something with the plow blade but wasn't sure what it was. He pumped the brakes to avoid a skid and came to a soft halt about twenty yards ahead of the point of impact. The snow was wild, stinging his cheeks and eyes as he moved, head to the wind, toward what he soon recognized as a black Audi sedan, stuck in a drift on the side of the road. He pulled the hood of his sweatshirt tight around his head to shield his face from the weather. He could hear a woman screaming before he actually saw her bent over something in front of the car. The red hazard lights on the car were flashing bright red, tinting the biting crystal flakes with a crimson glow as they swirled around the vehicle.

A man was lying face-down in front of the car, blood pooling around his head, staining the white snow scarlet. The woman was hysterical, screaming his name.

"Rob, look at me. Robert, it's Carly. Oh God, oh my God, he's dead. He's gone!"

She collapsed on the snow beside him, laying her head close to his face. The driver stood still, overwhelmed by the shocking scene in front of him. He was confused and frightened, knowing that he had caused the accident. His immediate reaction was to run away, but instead, he bent down and helped the woman to her feet. The taste of fear was metallic in his mouth.

"I didn't see him, lady. I couldn't see the car. The snow was blinding. I didn't see him. I'm so sorry. I'm so sorry. I didn't see him. You shouldn't have been on the road in this weather, lady. No one is out tonight. What were you thinking? What were doing out in this?" He had his arm around Carly's shoulder, holding her tightly to keep her standing. Overcome with shock, she leaned into him without looking at him or speaking to him.

A few cars were making their way slowly along the roadway, and they slowed to a halt once the drivers realized what had happened. The driver of the first car, an elderly man, parked about twenty feet behind the Audi and got out to see if he could help. The plow driver left Carly standing there, while he took the old man aside and asked him if he would call an ambulance for them. The man hurried back to his car and made the call on his cell phone, then grabbed a blanket from his backseat and rushed back, trailing the plaid blanket over his arm.

"Here, put this over him. I've got an ambulance coming. Is he conscious?" he asked.

"I think so, but we need to get him help soon. He's pretty badly hurt," the plow driver replied.

"What about the girl?" the old man asked.

"I think she's okay," the plow driver answered. "She's in shock but not hurt as far as I can tell."

"What happened?" the old man asked him.

"I don't know. I didn't see the car and was on it before I realized it was even there. I heard the plow blade scrape the side of the car, but so help me, God, I had no idea there was someone in the path of the blade."

THREE

Carly was shivering uncontrollably as she watched the life pour out of her fiancé into the snow piled around the car. The man beside her was holding her up, and in her dazed state, she thought that he must be the driver of the plow. His head was fully covered by the hood of his jacket, and he was hunched over so she couldn't see his face. The wind was so loud that she barely heard a word he was saying. He had his arm around her shoulders, and she thought she heard him say his name was Michael. Her only thought was to call her father, and she grabbed her cell phone from her pocket and dialed him.

Within a few minutes, the sound of sirens shattered the night. There was a police cruiser and an ambulance coming up on them, red and blue lights flashing in the snow. The vehicles stopped just behind the car, and the ambulance crew pulled the stretcher and security board from the rear of the truck. They checked Rob for vital signs and then covered his body with a blanket, placing him gently on a stretcher to lift him into the ambulance. The police took the driver of the truck into the cruiser as Carly followed the stretcher into the ambulance. A tow truck arrived and hooked the front end of the Audi up to load it onto the bed of the truck and haul it away.

It took almost twenty minutes to reach Massachusetts General Hospital. Carly held Rob's hand for the entire ride, feeling him slipping away as his hand grew icy cold in hers. She prayed, rocking back and forth. "Please, God, please, God, don't take him. Please let him be all right."

A priest was waiting at the emergency room entrance for the ambulance, and he administered the last rites as soon as the stretcher was inside the hospital door. Robert Emmet Shaw was pronounced dead on arrival at 12:10 a.m. of December 28.

Rob's parents had been called by the police and were waiting at the hospital when the ambulance brought him in. His mother collapsed onto the bench near the emergency room when she saw the EMTs bring the stretcher down the corridor. Carly went to sit with her while his father handled the paperwork. Carly's parents showed up within minutes of the ambulance's arrival. Hannah was near hysteria as she ran down the long corridor, her arms flailing in all directions and nearly tripping on her long coat. She was in her nightgown, and her hair was sticking out in long wisps from under her hat. George was stoic and expressionless as he followed his frantic wife. Carly didn't remember calling them, but she was relieved to see them and burst into tears as they approached her. Her father silently gathered her into his arms, and she buried her head into his shoulder, feeling strangely comforted by the wet, tweedy smell of his jacket. The three of them stood in the brightly lit hospital corridor, locked in solemn embrace.

The Boston police had sent two officers to the hospital to conduct a preliminary investigation.

"What happened, Ms. Richardson? Can you remember any of the detail?" one of them asked. Carly tried to reassemble what she remembered into something coherent.

"It happened so quickly, Officer, that I'm not exactly sure. Rob was trying to free the car from the snow bank and I heard a scraping sound and a sickening thud. I just remember kneeling in the snow beside him, calling his name. His head was in a pool of blood."

She stopped for a moment to catch her breath. The police officer was rapidly taking notes.

"Go on, Ms. Richardson. What else?"

Carly fought to hold back tears. She suddenly felt completely exhausted and grabbed her father's arm for support before she answered. "All the rest is a blur officer. I don't remember anything else."

"What you've told us agrees with what the driver of the truck has said. This was a very unfortunate accident, and I want to let you know that the driver has been taken to the police headquarters for questioning. Where can we reach you, Ms. Richardson, if we need to talk with you further?"

George spoke up before Carly could answer.

"She'll be with me and her mother, Officer. The phone number is on my business card."

George handed him a card and excused himself as he led his wife and daughter away, his arm still around Carly's shoulder.

The funeral service was held three days later in the midst of a steady, icy rain. Saint Mary's Cathedral was filled to capacity, and the archbishop of Boston, a longtime friend of Rob's family, presided at the High Mass. Over a hundred cars made their way to Saint Joseph's Cemetery in Brooklyn for the burial service. People were huddled together under umbrellas, shivering in the cold rain while the final prayers were said. Carly endured the entire process in a robot-like state, silently accepting the hugs and condolences from her friends and Rob's friends as they left the graveside services and headed their separate ways. Rachel stood at Carly's side the entire time, holding her hand tightly in her own, wishing she could ease her best friend's pain.

Hannah knew that Carly was nervous about going back to the apartment alone, so she coaxed her into staying at the family home in Lexington. Carly, still numb with grief, accepted the invitation with no argument. She hated the idea of having to stay with her parents and planned to go back to her own place in a few days. The days turned into weeks while Carly sat back and let her parents run her life.

Hannah liked nothing better than to be in control of things, and she took charge of Carly's situation with gusto. She fussed about the house with her notepad and pen in hand, writing constantly as she counted and recounted the wedding gifts that were strewn about the place. Carly sat back and watched as her mother, now on a self-appointed mission, put the crystal and linens into numbered and labeled little boxes and cartons. Hannah cataloged every gift and stored it all neatly away on metal shelves in the basement beside the boxes of old Christmas ornaments and the striped cushions for the lawn furniture. She hated clutter, and the effort was more for her benefit than for Carly's. She made endless trips to the basement, careful to protect her tidy little cotton dresses from the dust with an apron and her hands with floral-printed cotton gardening gloves. She made sure that her hair was tied back neatly, but every once in a while, Carly could see her pushing back some imaginary wisp of curl that she thought might have escaped its rubber-band prison. Rachel was there almost every day after work, and she teased Hannah about being the most perfectly dressed and coifed inventory manager she had ever seen. Hannah reacted predictably. "My dear girl," she said, "one never knows who will come calling at the door. It would be terribly embarrassing for me to be seen in those hideous dungarees you girls wear all the time. I prefer to dress properly even when I am doing housework. George might have an important client drop something off at the house, or someone from the country club might stop by to say hello. You just never know, dear. And I certainly don't want to be caught off guard."

George took full responsibility for all the insurance and legal issues, keeping Carly out of all of it. She, in turn, was glad to remove herself from the final details. He made sure that he was at the court hearing and was not surprised that the case was dismissed as an accident. The driver of the plow had his license suspended for six months, but that was the only penalty he had to pay. Carly never asked what happened, and George decided not to say anything to her until she did.

By the end of two weeks and after another series of trips back and forth to the basement, Hannah, with Rachel's help, had managed to return all the wedding gifts, accompanied by the appropriate explanatory notes. Carly offered to help, but they insisted that she just rest and let them do the work. She became a passive bystander to her own reorganization ceremonies, watching from the sidelines as if she were watching a movie. George remained noticeably absent from the business of rearranging his daughter. He grudgingly gave her a three-week leave of absence from the firm, reminding her every night of his generosity. Within a week, he had moved on from the tragedy and acted as if it never happened. Hannah knew that Carly was hurt and upset by his lack of sympathy and finally spoke with him about it after dinner one evening. Carly had asked to be excused from the table, giving Hannah the perfect opportunity.

"George, you are such a coldhearted old thing," she said. "Carly is grieving, and all you can say to her is that she's lucky she works for you so she could have the time off! It would be nice if you showed a little compassion to your daughter!"

"For heaven's sake, Hannah, she can't bring him back now, can she? She needs to move on with her life. All this crying and moping about aren't going to do any good. You baby her too much. She's a grown woman. If she doesn't start shaping up, she will have some unpleasant consequences," he replied.

"I think you should just stay out of it, George," Hannah shot back. "She doesn't need any of your sanctimonious lectures right now. What she does need is a hug from you, but you'd never think of doing anything like that, would you? Your daughter might actually think you are human!"

"Hannah, don't be ridiculous! The best thing she could do right now is get back to work and get her mind off this whole thing."

Hannah turned her back on him and walked out of the dining room.

Carly overheard the conversation and silently congratulated her mother for speaking up to him. His attitude was no surprise, and while Carly was hurt by his aloof demeanor, she completely expected it.

He had been that way with her all her life. He never gave her an inch on anything, and she insulated herself against his lack of warmth at a very young age. She told her mother once, after George had missed her birthday party, that she thought he wished she had never been born. Hannah immediately denied the accusation.

"How can you even think that, dear?" she had asked. "Look how hard your father works, and look at all the nice things you have! If he didn't love you, he wouldn't be doing all of this for you!"

"Mama, it's not always about *things*," Carly said. "He never listens to me about anything. I can't even ask him a question without his turning it into some sort of challenge for me so that I have to get the answer on my own. Just for once, I would like to have a real conversation instead of a challenge from him."

Hannah knew that Carly was right. George was unapproachable most of the time, and on the few occasions that they managed to have a conversation as a family, he would wave his intelligence around like a flag at them, cutting short any chance of a real dialogue at all. It was the George Richardson, Esq. show, and that was that!

Ordinarily, Carly could smile at her mother's eccentricities and shrug off her father's prodding, but as the weeks passed, she grew restless and her depression seemed to worsen. She lost interest in everything, forcing herself out of bed each morning to go to a job she had come to hate. She loved her parents dearly, but her mother's incessant chatter drove her crazy, and her father's constant reminders that work was piling up at the office forced her to think about going back to her own apartment in Cambridge. She had not tried to get any information about the driver of the plow truck in an effort to block the memory of the accident from her mind as much as possible. She remembered that his name was Michael, but she could not recall either his face or his voice, only that he had held her tightly in a blinding snowstorm while they watched her fiancé die at their feet. The accident haunted her. Her sleep was disrupted every night by vivid dreams of driving through snow, bitter cold, and sirens screaming above the howl of a northeast wind. The sensation of being trapped in deep snow woke her each time she dreamed.

Carly went through all the motions of her daily routine like a windup toy. She was exhausted from lack of sleep and found it difficult to function at full capacity. Her friends tried to be supportive, but even their attentions began to wane when she showed little enthusiasm for anything or anyone. Rachel called her almost every night and finally coaxed her to meet for a Sunday night dinner at a small Cambridge bistro. By the time Rachel arrived at the restaurant, Carly had already finished two glasses of wine. She watched as Rachel entered through the restaurant's glass doors, amused as some of the people turned to stare at the striking young woman with dark brunette hair and deep brown eyes. She had her hair tied back in a ponytail and was wearing a deep red wool coat and tall black leather boots. Carly waved to her as she made her way to the table.

Carly was a beautiful girl in her own right. She had inherited her mother's curly auburn hair and her father's green eyes. Like Rachel, she was tall and slender, and when they were together, they attracted admiring attention from everyone around them. But Carly didn't attract much flattering attention on that particular evening. She was pale, with dark circles under her eyes, and her curly hair was disheveled. Usually a fastidious dresser, her outfit was a thrown-together exercise suit and an old Harvard hoodie. Rachel's face was a dead giveaway that she was shocked at Carly's appearance.

"Sorry, I'm a little late," Rachel apologized. "How long have you been here?"

"I got here about forty-five minutes ago," Carly told her. "I had to get out of that house, so just thought I would get here early and have a drink while I waited."

Rachel looked at her friend, raising her eyebrows at the two empty wine glasses on the table. Carly had never been much of a drinker, and Rachel was surprised that she had put down two glasses of wine already. She sat down beside Carly and hugged her then leaned back and studied her face for a minute.

"I hate to be the one to tell you this, girlie, but you look terrible. Aren't you sleeping well?"

"Wow, thanks for the compliment! But you're right. I know I look awful. I hardly sleep at all, Rach. I go to bed and then keep having nightmares about the accident. And snow! Piles and piles of snow, snow falling all the time. I can't seem to shake them off. Not every night, but at least four or five times a week. I try taking sleep aids, warm milk, anything, but nothing seems to work. I'm exhausted and almost afraid to close my eyes. I'm thinking of making an appointment with Dr. Curtin just to get some sleeping pills or something."

"You need to do something, girlfriend. If you don't, you're going to end up sick!" Rachel said.

"I have decided to do one thing," Carly replied. "I'm going to move back to my own place sometime this week. My folks aren't terribly happy about it but I need to be on my own again, and I need to think about making some changes in my life. Going back to Cambridge will at least be a good start."

They finished their meals and Carly made the first move to leave, promising to call Rachel later in the week. What she didn't tell Rachel was that she was thinking of leaving her father's law firm and starting over with something entirely different.

Rachel watched her friend walk away, worried that Carly was in a deeper depression than she had originally thought. She hoped that a move back to her apartment might get her on the right track again.

FOUR

Carly was startled out of her daydream by a sharp knock on her office door. Her father entered the room without invitation and stood near the doorway, looking grimly at her. His annoyance was clearly imprinted in the frown that wrinkled his broad forehead.

"I see you are immersed in your work again, Carly," he said in his most sarcastic tone of voice. "Get your coat. I want to take you to lunch. Meet me in the lobby." Without waiting for a reply, he turned and walked towards the elevator. Carly, dreading the thought of another tirade from him, knew she had no choice but to join him. The wind and rain had picked up considerably and by the time they had walked across the street to the restaurant, their clothes were wet and they were shivering from the raw cold. They hadn't been seated for more than a minute when he started in on her.

"What are we going to do about you, Carly? You mope around with a dark cloud over your head all the time. Everyone is talking about it. You have got to snap out of this. The other partners are on my ass all the time about it. I can't keep making excuses for you."

"Dad, in case you haven't noticed, my life has been turned upside down. I can't just snap out of it!"

Her eyes filled with tears, and George suddenly wished that he hadn't started this conversation. He couldn't stand it when women cried in front of him. A weakness of character, he called it.

"Listen to me, Carly, your whole life is still ahead of you, and you have to start moving on. It's been almost four months now. Your mother and I are worried about you, and your friends have no idea what's going on with you. You have got to get on with life."

She wiped her eyes, hoping that no one had noticed her crying.

"I know. I know," she told him. "I'm thinking the best thing for me right now is a change. I am going to move back to my apartment this week, and I am also thinking that I want to get away from practicing law for a while, Dad. My heart isn't in it anymore, and I know you see that."

George was concerned for the first time that he might be losing his daughter from the firm and ultimately from his control. He had carefully mapped out her career, hoping that she would one day become a senior partner with him. He was the one who insisted that she go to Harvard, and he was the one who pushed her into Harvard Law School. This announcement was not in his grand plans at all.

"Okay. I can understand why you want to go back to your own place, but leaving the firm? That's foolish talk, Carly. Time will make things better. It's a normal reaction, and it's just going to run its course. Work is the best thing you can do, you know. What if I get you transferred out of the estate division and into corporate law? I know you hate working with those old biddies. If you went to corporate, you'd be working with a group of your fellow Harvard grads in that department!"

She looked at him, incredulous that he even mentioned this after what she just told him. "Dad, why can't you listen to me just once? You haven't paid attention to one thing I just said! You're so caught up in your own agenda that no one else matters. Did it even occur to you that I just might have some plans of my own?"

She was furious with him, raising her voice as she delivered her parting shot. People were beginning to stare, and she toned her voice down.

"You're so pigheaded sometimes. I don't know how my mother has put up with you all these years." She tore her coat from the back of her chair, ending both the conversation and the lunch as quickly as possible. "I'm going back to the office. I have a conference call in a little while. Thanks for lunch. I'll see you later." She walked away from the table before George had a chance to say another word.

The luncheon meeting was Carly's point of no return. By the time she got back to the office, she had made up her mind to make the changes that she hoped would let her get her life back. That afternoon, she contacted a local headhunter, and she began looking through the newspapers and on Craigslist for opportunities that would give her a fresh start. Within a week, she started sending résumés to all kinds of companies, trying to find a fit that would let her utilize her law school degree without actually working as a lawyer. She moved out of her parents' Lexington home that night and back into her own apartment in Cambridge, that she had shared with Rob. She had set the wheels in motion that would let her begin to pick up the pieces of her life and move on.

She hadn't changed her mind about leaving her father's law firm, but at least the time spent there would be more bearable. George didn't know for certain that she was planning on leaving, but he suspected that something was going on. He noticed over the next few weeks that she was on the phone more than usual and commented about it to Hannah.

"She's up to something, Hannah, I know she is," he said at dinner one evening.

"She never spends a lot of time on the phone, but lately, every time I go by her office, she has the phone stuck to her ear, and if she notices me, she pretends to be busy writing something or flipping through notebooks. I'm telling you, Hannah, something's going on with her."

"George, don't be so suspicious. Maybe she's just starting to get in touch with her friends again. God knows she needs to get out more. And I know that Rachel Ashe calls her a lot because she's been worried about her. There's probably nothing more to it, so stop worrying!"

"You mark my words, Hannah. There is something going on," he said, wagging his finger in her face. "You mark my words."

FIVE

B y the middle of July, Carly sent out over a hundred resumes and was beginning to get discouraged at the poor response to her barrage, thinking that she would have to resign herself to a life of tedious estate trust oversight and meetings with the dried-up old ladies who owned them. A few interviews materialized in June from the résumés that Carly had sent out, but she couldn't seem to connect with anything that suited her. The headhunter hadn't turned up anything worthwhile, and she was starting to get discouraged.

Then the letter came near the end of July from a small police department in northern Vermont. There was an immediate opening for a police officer to join the Saint Basile Department, and they wondered if she would be interested in arranging an interview.

The idea of living in Vermont intrigued her. It was far enough away from Boston to make the move worthwhile, and she had always loved the northern part of New England. She looked the town up on the Internet and was surprised at how far north it actually was—twenty miles from the Canadian border and located right on Lake Champlain. Burlington was less than an hour away. The population was under fifteen hundred, smaller than she would have liked but still worth a look. She contacted the Saint Basile Police Department and scheduled an interview to take place three days after the letter was received.

Telling her parents that she was considering the move would be traumatic. George had suspected for a while that she had been sending out résumés, but he never once believed she would actually leave the law firm. Carly wanted to talk with Rachel before she let her parents know and called her the day after she received the interview request.

"Rach, I need to run something by you. Got a couple of minutes?"

"I always have time for you, Carly. What's up?" she asked.

"I've decided that I'm definitely going to leave my job, and an interview has come up that I'm going to take. It's in Vermont, Rach, northern Vermont. This may be my chance to start over."

Rachel knew that Carly had wanted to leave the law firm, but like George, she never suspected that she would actually do it.

She told Rachel about the position and then waited for some sort of a response. Rachel was quiet for a minute, then she said, "Pretty dramatic change, Carly, but maybe you're right. Maybe that's what it will take. Look, you know I'll support whatever decision you make, but from a purely selfish point of view, I'll hate to see you move so far away."

"I know," Carly replied. "I have some mixed feelings about it too. It's also a drastic change from what I have been doing since I graduated. And I'll miss you terribly as well, but it's not *that* far away, and last I heard, you had a car! I don't have the job yet anyway, so let's not get too worried!"

"Have you told your folks yet?" Rachel asked.

"Not yet. I'm going to wait until tomorrow night just before I leave for the interview. That way, I won't have to listen to them yapping in my ear about the whole thing for days on end."

Rachel smiled to herself, picturing George and Hannah's response to this bit of news.

"I'd love to be a fly on the wall when you tell them," she said. "When do you think you'll drop the bomb?"

"I thought I'd have them to my place for dinner tomorrow night. Maybe I can ply them both with enough wine so that the shock of the news will be dulled."

They laughed, picturing the scene. "I can see it now," Rachel said. "George will be red-faced, puffing himself up to his most threatening posture. Your mother will be wringing her handkerchief in her hands, looking like the deer in the headlights."

Carly laughed again at the image.

"Rachel, I'll call you right after I tell them, I promise. Unless, of course, he kills me first!"

Carly called her mother as soon as she and Rachel hung up.

"Mama, how about you and Daddy coming to dinner tomorrow night? You haven't been here for a while and I thought it was time I invited you. What do you say?"

"I'll have to check with your father, dear, but I am sure it will be fine. Is there parking available there, or are we going to have to walk for miles? You know how your father hates to walk, and if he has to walk through those dirty streets, he will be in a foul mood by the time we get there."

"Don't worry, Mama. I will let you use my space right in front of the apartment building. Just be here around six thirty, okay?"

Hannah promised they would be on time, and Carly now had to plan exactly how she was going to break the news.

She set the stage by preparing her father's favorite meal, her mother's pot roast recipe. To her surprise, it turned out perfectly, but at the expense of a chaotic kitchen, with dirty bowls and pots and pans strewn over every countertop. George and Hannah arrived exactly on time, and Carly fixed each of them a Manhattan while she finished preparing the dinner. She could tell the minute they walked in that Hannah still disapproved of the apartment. She had never liked it and expressed her feelings about Cambridge every chance she got. Carly saw her wrinkle her nose up as if some foul odor had passed by her nostrils. But to her credit, Hannah didn't say anything, playing the role of the gracious guest to perfection.

The dinner conversation was pleasant enough, and everyone was careful not to bring up controversial issues. Hannah chattered aimlessly as usual about country club affairs, church committees, and her bridge club gossip. Carly pretended to pay attention, nodding yes or no as seemed fit. George stared at his wife the whole time in amazement at the way she could find so much to talk about things of so little interest to anyone but herself. They finished the main course, and Carly mustered up enough courage to start "the conversation" while they were having dessert. Silk sensed her tension and hid under the table with his head on her knee.

She took a deep breath, followed by gulp of wine.

"I have something interesting to tell both you. I'm going to Vermont tomorrow to interview for a job. I got a request for an interview from the Saint Basile's Police Department. The letter says they are very interested in me, and the position is open immediately."

Hannah sat bolt upright in her chair and looked at George. George stopped eating his pie, his fork in midair, and glared over his glasses with narrowed eyes. He slammed the fork down and leaned back in his chair, chin tucked in and arms folded across his chest.

"Go on," he growled. "What is this job that will take you from an excellent position in a prestigious law firm to a godforsaken frozen place like Saint Basile, Vermont?"

His face was crimson, and the blue veins at his temples were bulging. His mouth was drawn into a tight, disapproving line, and his soul-piercing stare cut through Carly like a spear.

She forged ahead, describing what she knew of the position. She tried to keep her voice steady as she spoke, but before she had a chance to finish, George interrupted her.

"A small-town police officer? That's the job? This is what you are doing with your Harvard Law School degree? Have you lost your bloody mind? Hannah, we have raised an idiot girl here."

Hannah, speechless and completely undone by Carly's announcement, looked from one to the other as if she were watching a Longwood tennis match.

George roared on, "Carly, if you go ahead with this, you will ruin your life and any chance of a successful career! And I will have nothing further to do with you. What a stupid, stupid thing to even consider." Still raging, he turned to Hannah. "This is all your fault, Hannah. You've ruined this girl with your ridiculous ideas and vapid advice. I knew something like this would happen sooner or later. I've been warning you about this for years!"

Hannah was silent, trying to look occupied by brushing imaginary crumbs off the tablecloth. George roared and blustered, pounding his fist on the dining room table until a wine goblet tipped over and broke, spilling red wine onto the white damask tablecloth. Silk scrambled for the bedroom, tail between his legs, ears flat back. Hannah sat rigid and red-faced in her chair, fussing with the pieces of broken goblet, trying to busy herself by mopping up the spilled wine with her napkin while George continued his tirade.

"Carly, if you are actually serious about this, then I am cutting you off immediately! Don't even bother to come to the office and get your things. I'll have Beth pack them up. I can't believe someone as smart as you could be so stupid!"

Carly was quiet, silently praying that her father would just shut up and listen. Finally, she cut in on him. "Dad, I am going to take that interview. I need to be doing what I want to do, not something that you want me to do."

She stood up, pacing back and forth, while she glared at him.

"I have to get away from here and start a new life. It's not good for me to stay. There is nothing for me here. I hate my job, and I don't want to practice law any longer. This may be a good opportunity, and I'm going to check it out. I'm very sorry that I don't want to be working in your law firm, advising rich old ladies about estate taxes. But I don't. And I *am* going to Vermont tomorrow morning for that interview."

She sat back down in her chair, trembling all over. Afraid to show her father how unnerved she was at his anger, she stood up again, picked up her plate, and marched indignantly into the kitchen with it. George and Hannah stayed at the table, staring at each other while Silk peered anxiously from the bedroom doorway, waiting until it was safe to come out. She stood at the sink, still trembling, but the sheer relief of having told them flushed over her, and she was suddenly overcome with an urge to burst into a fit of childish laughter. She covered her mouth with the dish towel, laughing soundlessly into it. She gradually composed herself and headed back to the dining room just as George was putting on his coat and helping Hannah with hers. He marched to the door without looking back and shouted to his wife, "Hannah, are you coming?"

Hannah moved nervously toward Carly.

"Dear, the dinner was lovely. I am so sorry about the wine spill. I know how to fix that. Try a little Borax on it, and then—"

She was stopped in midsentence as George grabbed her by the arm and led her out of the apartment.

Carly called Rachel immediately as promised.

"Well, I did it! I told them!"

"Oh my God, Carly. What did they say? Did your father explode?" Rachel asked.

"He was apoplectic! Red-faced, yelling, pounding, growling. He reminded me of a raging old bull walrus! And my mother… she was speechless, scared I think. He broke one of my wine glasses, and the wine spilled all over the place. Mother spent the entire time picking at the pieces and trying to mop up the spill. I'm not sure, but I think I got disowned!"

"I bet your mother will call me to try to knock some sense into you," Rachel said. "She's probably trying to reach me right now.

Carly, I have to tell her that I think what you're doing is a really good idea. She won't like it, but I don't want to be dishonest."

"Let me know if she does call you, Rach. I'll be curious to hear what she has to say. I'm leaving in the morning, and I'll call you in a couple of days. I might just stay up there through the weekend. It will be good to get away, and if something terrific happens, I promise you'll be the first to know!"

Rachel thought that Carly sounded like her old self for the first time in months and hoped that things would turn out well for her in that interview. Five minutes after she hung up with Carly, Rachel received the expected call from Hannah.

"Rachel? It's Hannah Richardson, dear. I'm so upset with Charlotte that I had to call you to see if you can talk some sense into her."

"What's the problem, Mrs. Richardson? I just spoke with Carly and she seemed fine."

"Then you don't know, dear? Oh my. We had such a terrible fiasco at her place tonight. I can barely even talk about it. She's going off to northern Vermont on some silly interview with a police department! Can you imagine? What has happened to that girl? George is beside himself with it all, and she won't listen to me. I wish you would call her, dear, and talk her out of this foolishness before she just ruins her life! She always listens to you, Rachel. Be a good girl and call her for us."

"Oh, *that* news! Yes, I did know about it, Mrs. Richardson. Carly told me about the interview."

"Well, I certainly hope you discouraged her, Rachel. This is such a mistake, such a mistake."

"Well, not exactly. I actually told her I thought it was a great idea. She's been miserable, and I think it would do her good to get out of here, you know, a whole change of environment and everything."

Rachel could hear Hannah sputtering at the other end.

"I had hoped we could count on you, Rachel, to talk some sense into her. I must say I am surprised and terribly disappointed that you are encouraging this," Hannah said.

Not wanting to take the conversation any further, Rachel pretended that she had another call coming in.

"Mrs. Richardson, I really have to go. I have a business call on my other line. I'm sure Carly will be just fine. You worry about her too much. I'll talk to you soon. Bye!"

Rachel hung up, leaving Hannah with her mouth open at the other end of the line. As she had promised, she called Carly to let her know that Hannah had contacted her.

"She was really furious, Carly. I felt sorry for her."

"Yeah, I know what you mean. I felt sorry for her, too, especially since she had to go home with him all in a snit."

"Maybe you should have told him you were thinking of leaving, Carly. It might have softened the blow. Know what I mean?"

"I thought about it, Rach, but my life wouldn't have been worth two cents if I had. I would have had both of them on my case about it. At least this way, it's done and over. If I do get this job, they might take the news a little better."

Rachel laughed at that remark.

"You must be dreaming, Carly. If you thought last night was bad, you haven't seen anything yet."

"I don't care, Rachel. I'm going, and I am going to make a good impression on that police captain. He'll have to hire me!"

SIX

C arly left Boston at six the next morning with a small suitcase and her dog and headed west on the Massachusetts Turnpike, then north toward Vermont. George called her cell phone several times, but she ignored the calls. There were five messages from him, all pleading with her to reconsider her "rash and incredibly stupid" decision. Hannah left just one message, but it was the equivalent of several.

"Carly, please call me when you get this message, dear. Your father is so upset with you, and I am so disappointed that you have gone and done something foolish like this. I just can't imagine why you would want to be a police officer in some backwater town in Vermont when you had a perfectly good job here at your father's firm. And by the way, did you manage to get the red stains out of your tablecloth? If you didn't, I came across a wonderful recipe for a stain remover, which I can tell you about. And I hope you got all that glass picked up. Your poor dog might step on a sliver if you missed any of it. Just vacuum. Much better than sweeping. And do call me, dear."

She ignored her mother as well.

Saint Basile was a good five-hour ride from Boston, and Carly left early to avoid the traffic on the Mass Pike during the morning rush hour. She had studied the map of northern Vermont, and Saint Basile was about as far north as one can get before crossing the border into Canada. The population was very small, and its saving grace was that it sat right on Lake Champlain, with Burlington not too far south. It was famous for its maple sugar production and its small-town congeniality, but not much else. By the time she crossed the state line from Massachusetts into

Vermont, Carly began to have serious second thoughts. She looked over at the dog curled up on the passenger seat.

"What do you think, Silk? Am I nuts like Father said? I don't know a thing about what cops do. I know one thing…Daddy was really furious. Maybe I really messed up this time."

Silk looked at her for a moment, his brown eyes intent on her face, then he licked her hand and turned his attention back to the open window. He stuck his head out, and the wind pushed his long ears back against his head and filled his mouth with air, pulling his jowls back into what Carly was sure was a smile.

Route 89 was a long snake of a road that crawled in and out of the Vermont hills and valleys. Carly kept the car windows open, feeling exhilarated by the smog-free air. She felt herself beginning to unwind, and the further away she got from Boston, the more relaxed she felt. She made a stop in Burlington to walk Silk and stretch her own legs. There was a small sandwich shop with some outside picnic tables near the roadside rest area where she picked up a sandwich and a hot coffee and coaxed the waitress into letting her take a small bowl of water for Silk. There were still about forty miles to go before she reached Saint Basile, but there was plenty of time before her interview, so she lingered at the little picnic table for a short while after she finished her lunch. She had been having second thoughts about her decision during the ride, and at one point she had considered turning back. She was filled with self-doubt about her ability to start over in a new job and a new place, afraid that she would fail miserably at both endeavors, but the thought of turning back into the old life was motivation enough to keep her moving forward. She wrapped up the remains of her lunch, determined to put the past aside. Before heading out on the highway again, she texted Rachel to let her know that she had made it to Burlington.

SEVEN

The Saint Basile Police Department was becoming too small for the growing town. There were two call officers, a captain, and a lieutenant. Jack McIntyre had been the police captain in Saint Basile for twenty years and had hired and trained dozens of new officers during his watch. He was on the verge of retirement and had been grooming his lieutenant, Scott Eames, to take over for him. Jack wasn't in the office very often, mostly because of some health issues that had left him partially disabled. For the first time in his career, he was having to consider hiring a woman. He had nothing against female police officers, but there had never been a female applicant during his time on the force and he was unsure about how to handle the impending interview. The population had doubled since the time Jack started, and he was being forced to make a hire by the board of selectmen. His poor health and pending retirement made the decision a little easier, and he hoped that Charlotte Richardson was everything her résumé said she was.

Over a hundred résumés came in from the search firms, but the one from the young Massachusetts girl intrigued him. She was an honors graduate from Harvard Law School and a practicing attorney. She was certainly overqualified, but her application letter made her almost impossible to overlook. She had written an ambitious and eloquent explanation as to why she should be considered for the job, and when Jack went over the résumé with Scott, they both agreed that they should at least meet her. There was some lengthy discussion about how well the town would take to a female law enforcement officer, but they decided not to worry about that at the moment.

"Putting the cart before the horse, that's what that is," Jack said. "Let's not come to any hasty conclusions."

On the morning of the interview, they were still talking about it.

"Scott, I am really on the fence about this. This isn't a great job for a single gal," Jack said.

"This isn't a great job for anybody," Scott replied. "The pay stinks, and there's nothing to do around here except maybe some hunting and fishing. Why would she want to come all the way up here anyway? I bet there is something wrong with her. I bet she's ugly. Or maybe she is running away from something. If that's true, I guess this would be a great place to hide!"

"I have no idea why she is interested, but I guess we'll find out when she gets here," Jack said. "Gotta admit I'm kinda curious to meet her anyway."

Carly arrived in Saint Basile Vermont on the first of August around noon and checked in at Knapps' Bed-and-Breakfast at the edge of town. It was a beautiful Mansard Victorian set back from the road on a lush green lawn. Willow trees lined the long walkway, their swaying branches forming a moving archway. The proprietor, Rita Knapp, was waiting on the front porch for her. They exchanged greetings, and Rita assured her once again that pets were welcome. "As long as you don't let him run loose around the inn!" she told Carly in a stern tone. She was a brittle stick of a woman with hawk-like eyes set in a thin, pinched face. *Mom would call her a prim and proper Yankee*, Carly thought.

Carly thanked her, making sure to keep Silk very close to her side.

"Let me show you around, Ms. Richardson," Rita said.

Carly put Silk in the fenced-in yard while she got a formal tour of the inn. The place was old and looked as if it had been restored back to its original woodwork and wallpaper. There were two formal sitting rooms, a large dining room, and a long galley-style kitchen, complete with an old soapstone sink and a cast iron and enamel stove. They walked in silence from room to room, which made Carly uncomfortable. She finally engaged her hostess in a conversation.

"This place is lovely, Mrs. Knapp. Did you and your husband do the restoration yourselves?" Carly asked.

"We had some help, but yes, for the most part, we did it all. It took three years to get it finished, but I think the effort was worth it. Our guests seem to love it, and a lot of them come back every year in the fall for leaf peeping," she replied in a dry voice.

Carly brought Silk in whey they finished the downstairs tour, and they followed Mrs. Knapp through one of the formal parlors to a beautiful, curved wooden staircase carpeted in a worn Oriental runner.

When Mrs. Knapp showed Carly her room, she felt as if she were stepping into a watercolor painting. Chintz curtains and bedding with floral patterns in soft blues and violets dominated the small area. Fresh hydrangeas had been placed in a clear vase near the window—entirely different from the Pottery Barn décor that she and Rob had so loved in their apartment. There was a small desk and a huge sky-blue armchair with down pillows set near the window.

"I'll just leave the key with you, Ms. Richardson. If you need anything at all, I'll be in the kitchen," Mrs. Knapp said. "We serve breakfast from six until nine in the morning, but not a minute later. There is always tea and coffee on the dining room sideboard in the afternoon. Usually some muffins and cookies too."

"Thanks very much," Carly replied. "I'll be leaving in about forty-five minutes. Just want to take a quick shower and change. I have an interview this afternoon."

"That's nice, dear. Where are you interviewing?" Mrs. Knapp asked.

"At the police department. I applied for the open officer's position, and I'm meeting Captain McIntyre about it today."

Mrs. Knapp's eyebrows raised, and Carly noticed that her mouth had tightened into a thin little line. She turned stiffly to head back down the stairs.

"Well, I hope things go well for you, dear. Do let me know how it turns out."

Silk settled into a spot of sunlight near the window while Carly showered and changed into her business suit. When she finished dressing, she put Silk's leash on him, and they headed down the staircase. As they passed the kitchen, she called out to her hostess, "I'm leaving now, Mrs. Knapp. Be back in a couple of hours. My dog is with me. Thanks for everything."

Rita Knapp waited until Carly pulled her car out of the driveway before she began dialing the phone. She tapped her fingers on the desk impatiently while she waited for someone to answer her call.

"Peg? It's Rita," she whispered into the phone. "You'll never guess what Jack McIntyre has gone and done! He's interviewing a young woman for that open position! Can you imagine? What in the world is he thinking?"

Within an hour, half of Saint Basile's population knew about the young woman from Boston, and rumors began to spread like wild fire.

EIGHT

C arly started out for the interview a little early so that she could see some of the town. The weather was cool but sunny for August, with a crisp blue cloudless sky. She opened all the car windows, savoring the refreshing feel of the air. Silk poked his head out of the passenger side window, loving the wind in his face and the thousands of new smells and sounds coming at him as they passed through the town. His nostrils flared and quivered as he tried to capture and identify each new smell. Carly liked Saint Basile instantly. There was a peaceful quality about the place, and she felt comfortable in a way that she hadn't felt in a long time. It felt like home.

She worked her way down Main Street and saw the police department building at the far end. It was an old wood-framed, single-story building set in front of a large tract of unused pastureland that ended at the edge of a heavily wooded area. The building was desperately in need of paint and a new roof, and it looked tired and worn. Some old oak trees lined the sidewalks in front of the building, and there was an ancient oak tree on the lawn that hid most of the front of the building from view. The rear of the building housed a two-cell jail block and a small garage with an attached workshop. A cluster of tall pine trees formed a thick forest in the land immediately behind the building, some of them looking as if they were ready to collapse with old age. All the windows on the building were encased in heavy black iron bars.

Carly parked her car in a space on the street and sat for a minute, fussing with her hair before getting out of the car and heading for the main entrance. She left all the windows open just a crack so that Silk could get some fresh air while she was gone.

She was nervous and her palms were sweaty, but she walked to the main door with a confident stride, hoping that her anxiety wouldn't show during the interview.

The reception area was small, paneled in dark pine slats, and furnished with old mismatched chairs and a relic of a sofa. Some sepia pictures of old farm scenes hung on the walls, most covering long-forgotten cracks in the plaster. A black cast-iron wood-burning stove sat in a corner of the room, with an old kettle resting precariously on the small, round stove top.

A good-looking uniformed man was working at the front desk. His desk plate said Scott Eames, Assistant Chief of Police. He stared at Carly for a minute before rising, his surprise obvious at the appearance of an attractive young woman standing by his desk. He got up and moved around to the front of his desk to greet her, his eyes never leaving her face.

"Ms. Richardson, I'm Lieutenant Eames," he greeted her as he reached out to shake her hand vigorously. "Good to see you, good to see you! I'll go get Captain McIntyre. He's in his office, I think. Have a seat, and he'll be right with you."

Carly watched him with interest. He was probably in his midforties, tall, with a full crop of dark hair that was graying at the temples. His shoulders were broad, and he was in what she and Rachel would consider "in good shape." She hadn't given a thought to anyone other than Rob in months, but there was something about this man that momentarily peaked her interest.

Before Carly could say a word, Scott headed toward the glass door at the rear of the room, nearly tripping over his own feet. She smiled, realizing that her presence had caused the fumbling misstep. She adjusted her jacket and skirt one more time then sat down on the wooden bench under the window. Scott opened the door to the large office and announced her arrival. "Jack, Charlotte Richardson is here."

She heard another man grunt back a remark and a door close. Captain Jack McIntyre, all 250 pounds of him, suddenly appeared, filling the doorway to the reception area with his six-foot-three frame. Carly stood up when he finally walked toward her and introduced herself.

"Captain McIntyre, I'm Charlotte Richardson," she said, extending her hand. "But everyone calls me Carly. I'm so pleased to meet you."

"Well, we're pleased to have you visit us, Carly," he said, flashing a broad smile. Like Scott, Jack was also pleasantly surprised that this applicant was so attractive. He wasn't quite sure what he expected, but Charlotte Richardson certainly wasn't it.

"Why don't you follow me to my office so we can have a chat," he said and escorted her to the glass door, opening it for her to enter ahead of him.

They talked for over an hour, with Jack going into great detail about the nature of the position, the compensation package, and the challenges that she would face as a new officer. Jack wanted to make sure that she was clear on all the details of her training requirements as well.

"Carly, I hope you understand that all of this is contingent upon your completing the training course at the Vermont Police Academy. I'm going to register you for the part-time course so that you can get your practical field work in at the same time. I wouldn't normally do it this way, but we are in a bit of a bind. What that means is that you will be a part-time officer here for a short period of time. We'll make sure you get moved up to the full-time slot immediately. You'll be on the job full-time but just not classified as full-time. That will change when you graduate. You'll have to take the entrance exam next week and then take the fifty-eight hour course, followed by fifty hours of elective courses. The sixty hours of field work can start as soon as you finish up those first three requirements. Overall, it will take you about three and a half weeks, tops."

She took in all the information, making copious notes about schedules and daily routines. After an hour of conversation, Jack leaned back in his swivel chair, staring intently at her.

"Carly," he said, "I must confess that I have some real concerns about a woman, especially a young attractive woman, taking this position. No offense, please, but this is the first time that this town has had a female applicant for a police officer's position. Some of the old-timers are not going to be receptive to the idea at all, and I am not sure how the board of selectmen will react. Saint Basile is a pretty quiet town as you've probably guessed. We have had our share of 'situations' in the past, which have been difficult even for us old-timers. But I don't think you will have to worry too much about real, serious stuff. One thing I would like to know from you is how you feel about some of the challenges you'll be facing. This is a far cry from the work you have been doing. I think you know what I'm referring to."

There it was. The question she knew would pop up before the meeting was over. The one she had been thinking about since she left Boston.

She had been concerned that there would be some gender bias surrounding this opportunity, and she had thought about how she would handle the issue.

"I've given this a lot of thought too, Captain. Honestly, I've had some second thoughts myself. This isn't like anything I have ever done in the past, and I had thought that a female officer might pose some problems in a small town like this. But I'm pretty good at dealing with challenges and difficult situations. I'm working in a law firm that is predominantly composed of male lawyers. I had to really prove myself with that bunch before I got to handle some of their high-profile accounts. It took a little while, but I was able to overcome the concerns of even the crustiest old partners. I can't imagine that Saint Basile's elders would even come close to the resistance I got from the old timers at the firm who thought that women were hired to do filing and copying and nothing else!"

She looked him directly in the eye now, feeling more confident as she spoke. "There'll be a learning curve for me, that's for sure, but I think the best way to do well at this job is to just dig in and learn everything I can about the town, the people, and the work. This is the same thing I had to do when I joined the law firm. If you're willing to give me the time to learn, I'm willing to do what it takes to succeed."

He liked her answer and nodded in agreement.

"The job would be a challenge for any new person," she continued. "And I'm aware that it may be a greater challenge for a woman. I'm very good at holding my own in tough circumstances, so I'm going to assure you that I'm up for it!"

Carly was certain that she gave the right response because she could tell by his body language that he had listened carefully. They chatted on for another half hour, but she sensed that Jack had made up his mind. She knew he'd make her an offer. He stood up, almost as if he had read her thoughts.

"I hope I am not going to regret this, Carly, but I think you would do an excellent job here, and I am willing to take a chance on you. I'm offering you the patrolman's position, and I hope you'll accept the offer. This is of course all subject to your passing the training requirements at the Police Academy in Burlington."

Carly wanted the job and didn't hesitate with her answer. "I'd love to work here, and thank you so much for the offer. Of course I'll accept it, and I promise you I will meet and even exceed the requirements," she replied.

She was grinning from ear to ear as they shook hands and headed out to the front office. Jack was beaming when they entered the room.

"Scott, I have good news! Carly, has accepted our offer and is starting immediately. I want you to take her over to Jed Moore at the real estate office and see if he can find her an apartment or a condo to rent. And by the way, pets have to be accepted. Tell Jed the town will pick up the first month and the security deposit for her. And tell him to find a decent place."

Scott was not sure if he should be happy about this turn of events, but he hid his uncertainty well.

"No problem, Jack. Carly, come along with me and let's see if we can get you settled someplace in the next day or two," he said.

"What made you decide to schedule an interview with us, Carly? This seems light-years away from what you have been used to."

"You're right, Scott. It is light-years away, but I think I was just ready for a change. My father is a senior partner in the law firm, and I really needed to get away and do something without his influence. I don't think he is going to be happy about this, but I don't really care. I'm very excited about the job and can't wait to get started."

Scott listened to her intently. Carly could tell that he was wondering how all of this was going to work out for him. He had never worked with a woman before and wasn't quite sure that he would be able to do so. But he liked her, she could tell, and that was half the battle. He opened the door of her car for her and asked her to follow him to the real estate office.

"The real estate office is just a few blocks away, Carly. I'm pretty sure they'll be able to find something for you."

Jack watched them head out to Main Street and congratulated himself on the positive outcome of the interview. He leaned back in his chair, feet up on the desk, and smiled at the way things turned out. He liked the young lawyer from Massachusetts. Carly Richardson was completely at ease during the interview, answering every question thoughtfully and asking some good questions in return. He knew she was a very intelligent young woman, and he had a feeling that she and Scott would get along very well. She would need some training, that was for sure, especially with firearms. She also knew the law, and he had no worries about her in that area. He felt at ease for the first time in months, satisfied that things would continue on smoothly and that the selectmen would be happy that the position was filled. He worried a little about how Scott would take to working with a very attractive young woman, but he had a feeling that things would work out just fine. He told Carly that he was planning on taking a medical leave of absence some time in the next few weeks, thinking that this information was something she needed to know. She had not expressed any concerns and seemed comfortable with the fact that Scott would take the captain's place when Jack finally did retire.

Scott returned to the office about an hour later.

"Well, we found her a nice condo for rent, Jack. Not too far from here. She seems like a nice girl. Smart, that's for sure. I think she'll work out just fine," he said. Jack grinned at him.

"Yup. I think she is perfect for the job. I also think that you two will work well together. The interesting part is going to be how the townies take to her. This is a real change for them. Scott, before I forget, give Jim a call and tell him we have hired a full-time officer, will you?"

"Sure," Scott replied. "Can't wait to hear his comments! And by the way, Jack, I am perfectly okay with this. Just in case you're wondering."

After finding the apartment, Carly drove around the town for a while. There were clusters of old Colonial-style homes near town commons, a typical New England scene, but beyond the center of town, the number of homes dwindled to a few farmhouses, most set apart by several acres of fenced pastureland. The town bordered Lake Champlain, and she followed a sign that indicated a shore route along the lake. About a half mile down on the shore road, there was a public beach and a boat-launching ramp. She parked the car on the side of the road and got out to let Silk have a run along the beach. There was an old wooden bench set back about fifty feet from the water's edge, and she sat for a while, watching the dog running in and out of the water as she tossed sticks for him to retrieve. The afternoon sun was warm, and she relaxed, enjoying the chance to be away from everything and by herself for a little while. She had promised to call Rachel if anything "exciting" happened but decided to wait until that evening, wanting to savor the peace of the late afternoon while she could.

By four o'clock, the trees had started to cast long shadows across the grass and sand along the water's edge, and the air was turning cool. Carly headed back to town, planning to grab a quick dinner at the bay pub, and then spend a quiet evening reading. When she arrived back at the inn, Mrs. Knapp was cutting hydrangeas in the front garden. She was wearing a wide-brimmed floppy straw hat and overalls, and she reminded Carly of a garden scarecrow she had seen once when she was little.

She called her mother first, and Hannah's reaction was totally predictable—questions and admonitions about her incredibly bad decision.

"Charlotte, for heaven's sake, how will you ever make any money at a job like that? And the weather is so terrible there in the winter. And what about your law degree? I just had a feeling you were going to take that job! Your father is so disappointed. Have you talked to him yet? Do you have a place to live yet? I suppose you will be in some sordid little apartment over a smelly fast-food restaurant. What about poor Silk in that awful winter weather? I can't imagine what would make you do something like this, dear. And you will probably never get back home to see us. What am I going to tell my bridge club, dear? That my lawyer daughter is now just a police officer? And carrying a gun, too, I suppose! I simply do not understand you at all. And you know how I feel about guns, dear. I have to tell you, Charlotte, I am *very* disappointed in you right now."

Hannah finally stopped talking in order to catch her breath, and Carly jumped in before the diatribe started up again.

"Mama, it really is okay. I've found a very nice little unit in a small condominium building. My furniture will be shipped here, and it will fit perfectly. The pay isn't *that* bad, and I will be fine here. Silk has plenty of space to run, and he won't mind a little snow. Just be happy for me, would you, please, for once in my life? I have a chance to start out fresh and put a lot of bad stuff behind me. It's a lovely town, and I know you would really like it. Lots of old homes and antiques and stuff like that."

She heard Hannah suck in her breath in disapproval.

"Well, if this is what you want, dear, then who am I to tell you what to do? Call your father."

And with that, Hannah hung up.

The call to George was far worse. When his secretary answered the phone, Carly tried to get an assessment of his mood. "Beth, it's Carly. What's his temperature today?"

"He just walked in from court, Carly," Beth replied, "so I haven't had a chance to test the waters yet. Do you want me to put you through?"

She thought about saying no but instead told Beth to connect her, hoping for the best and expecting the worst.

"Hello, Dad," she chirped when he picked up the phone. "Just thought I would give you a call and tell you my news."

Silence.

"Dad, are you there?"

She could hear him breathing into the speaker, and she had a flashing image of his tanned face all knotted up, his bushy eyebrows meeting in a frown, and his eyes glaring over his half spectacles in grim disapproval.

"I'm here," he grumbled. He adjusted his glasses and ran his hand through his thick gray hair in frustration. "I suppose you're calling to tell me you took that goddamn job in Vermont."

"Well, yes, as a matter of fact, I did take it. I'll start right away. They are going to train me and everything. And the pay is pretty good too. And I love it up here. The town is lovely, and I'm close to the lake and to all the ski trails too. I have found a great rental unit with a big yard for Silk. You and Mother should plan to come up and visit me when I get settled. Dad, I'm sorry for the short notice. This is just something I have to do for myself right now."

She chattered on nervously until he stopped her short.

"Carly, stop that blathering. You sound just like your mother! And by the way, did you call your mother?"

"Yes, I talked to her about an hour ago."

"And…what did she say?"

"Oh, you know how Mama is. She went on and on about a hundred things, and I could barely get a word in. She really just kept asking a lot of questions."

She could hear him drumming his thick fingers on the leather top desk and knew this conversation wasn't going anywhere.

"Well, Carly, I am neither going to ask you a lot of questions nor make any further comments at all. You know my feelings about this. I have made myself perfectly clear to you. There is nothing more to be said."

He slammed the receiver back in its cradle.

"Great," she said to Silk. "I have just had both parents hang up on me in the space of two hours."

Carly dialed Rachel's number, hoping to get a better response from her than she did from her parents. The voice mail came on, and Carly, disappointed that Rachel didn't answer, left a message.

"Rach, it's me. Guess what? I got the job and I start right away, and I found a great little condo to rent. The town is beautiful! I'm happy, *happy*. Please call me back on my cell phone and please come up here as soon as you can. You'll love it too!"

Rachel called back within an hour, anxious to hear what Carly had to say.

They chatted for a while and ended up with Rachel promising a visit right after Labor Day.

Carly's furniture arrived from Boston two days later, and she checked out of the inn and settled in to her new place. Her training classes started later that week, filling every spare minute of her time. She had to scramble to find a place for Silk during the day while she was in Burlington and ultimately arranged for a kennel just outside town to take him during the daytime hours. By mid-August, she was fully involved at the police academy. There were ten other trainees from various towns in Vermont, all hoping to pass the series of tests they would have to take. Carly felt overwhelmed at times, surprised at how much there was to learn. After she completed the entrance exam requirements, she started with the firearms courses, beginning with pistol and then moving to the rifle. Most of the elective courses were about the law, and she breezed through those without problem. What surprised her most was that she found that she actually liked using the guns, and by the end of the month, she had completed the course, almost reaching expert level with both rifle and pistol. The written exams were easier for her, and she passed with high grades on all of them. A few of the fitness courses were pretty tough, but she made it through all of them with passing grades.

There was one other female trainee in the classes, but she dropped out midway into the program, unable to pass the fitness tests. Carly was determined that she would finish every course no matter how difficult it might be. There were days when she could barely make the trip back to Saint Basile's from Burlington. She was exhausted physically and mentally and collapsed into bed by seven o'clock every night. She felt guilty that she had very little time to spend with Silk when she got home, and to make matters worse, she was lonely. She kept telling herself that all this would change once she had graduated from the training academy. The graduation exercises were scheduled for the Labor Day weekend, and she crossed the days off the calendar on her kitchen wall like a child waiting for Christmas.

NINE

Rachel called Carly on the Thursday before Labor Day with bad news.

"I have to cancel my trip up there this weekend, Carly," she said. "My sister had her baby yesterday, two weeks early, and she asked me if I could stay with her over the weekend. I couldn't say no. I'm so sorry. I know you were looking forward to this weekend. So was I. I promise I'll make it up to you."

Carly was greatly disappointed by Rachel's call, but she knew that Rachel felt badly about cancelling, so she tried to make light of it.

"Don't worry, Rach. We can do it some other time. You need to stay with Maggie. Tell her I said congratulations and give her a hug for me, okay?"

"Thanks for understanding, Carly. I'll be up there the first chance I get."

"I know you will, Rachel. No worries," Carly told her. "The wine and cheese won't go bad, I promise."

Carly graduated with honors from the police academy, and with training behind her, she was able to get some real on-the-job experience by shadowing Jack or Scott in the patrol truck or doing church or town event special details on the weekends. Silk was always with her, and just about everyone stopped to give him a pat and a treat. Carly made it a point to get to know as many of the townspeople as she could, and Scott saw to it that she attended all the Little League and Pop Warner games in her free time so the kids would see that she was showing an interest in them. Initially, the townspeople were apprehensive about her, but after a few weeks, she felt their discomfort easing. The old-timers especially went out of their way to make conversation with her, and it didn't take long before she knew almost everyone by first name.

She made no attempt to contact her parents again, hoping that a "cooling off period" would settle things down. Hannah left a few messages for her, but Carly ignored them. She and Rachel talked a couple of times a week, but Rachel's work schedule wouldn't free her up to visit until mid-October, much later than Carly would have liked. Carly missed her and some of her other friends as well. She tried to keep busy on her days off, but the camaraderie that she enjoyed just a few months ago in Boston was missing, and she hated to admit it to herself that she felt homesick. The residents of Saint Basile were all nice enough, but there didn't seem to be too many single people that she could hang out with when she had time off. They were all either married and raising kids or involved with their own careers, most of them working in Burlington every day.

Carly knew that Captain McIntyre expected her to be on her own by early October, which was beginning to worry her. Her confidence level was like an elevator—one minute up, one minute down, with some stops in between. She continued to shadow Scott, but she worried constantly about her ability to do it alone and do a good job. She had a full-blown confidence crisis going on, and for the first time since she took the job, she began to feel entirely out of her comfort zone. Day by day, a little worm of fear chewed at her, and she expressed some of her worry about full duty to Scott at lunch one day. He had been watching her and knew something was bothering her. He'd wanted to talk with her but held back, sensing that she wasn't ready to share a confidence with him just yet. He gave her an opening just as they were finishing lunch.

"So, Carly, how are things going so far? We've talked about everything except the job. Are you getting comfortable with things?"

His question took her by surprise.

"Well, generally I think things are going fine, but…" She stopped, not sure if she should go any further.

"But what?" he asked. "You can tell me. I'm really a good listener."

"I feel like a fool talking you about this," Carly said. "It's just that this is so different from anything I've done before. I know I'll be okay, but every once in a while, the doubt demons would start whispering in my ear, and then I begin to wonder if I made the right decision. I'm not sure I really could handle a serious crime, you know. I just don't know if I'm cut out to do that kind of stuff. It's so different from working in a law firm, and I do so want to do a good job. Part of my problem is that I have something to prove to my parents, as well as to myself. Guess I am just putting a lot of pressure on myself because of it."

Scott listened attentively to her, feeling sorry that she was having a rough time.

"I think you're worrying too much," he said. "Listen, I've seen a lot of people come and go over the years here, mostly city folks who don't do well in the harsh winters. Some of them tend to move on after a couple of years. Most just pack up and head out after the first winter. A few stick it out and try to make a go of it. I don't think you need to be concerned. This is a pretty quiet town. Not a lot of dangerous stuff going on here. You're going to be just fine. And besides, I'm right here beside you to help if you need it."

Scott had the kind of personality that put people at ease right away, and Carly relaxed, grateful to him for listening.

"Scott, I'm sorry I bothered you with this," she said. "But I just have no one up here to talk to. Gets lonesome sometimes. Thanks for listening, and I do appreciate your offer. Really, I do."

"You know," he said, "I just met the family that bought the old Lakeview Farm last fall. Malone's the name I think. Nice couple. Moved up here from your neck of the woods. You should get out there one of these days and say hello. I think the wife is around your age. I don't know too much about her husband. Met him just once, but I hear that he's a real loner. Jack met him and thinks that he acts as if he has a secret or something. Hard to explain, but you can come to your own conclusions when you meet them. I really think you will like her. She seems to be very outgoing, and I know people in town like her. You might just make a new friend!"

They finished lunch and headed out of the diner toward the patrol truck. Carly took Scott's hand in hers.

"Thanks again for listening, Scott. I know I can do this. I will definitely make a point to meet the Malones. It would be nice to start making some new friends here."

She made a mental note to ride out to Lakeview Farm later that week.

Scott dropped her off at the police station and headed back out to check on an earlier disturbance call. He understood exactly how Carly felt. He was the same way when he first got to Saint Basile. He had been married for three years when his wife was stricken with cancer and died after a long battle with the disease. There were no children, and there was nothing to keep him in Connecticut, where he was the police chief in a small town in the western part of the state. He stayed on simply because it was comfortable and predictable. After a couple of years, he grew restless and started looking for a position that would give him a fresh start in a place where there were no sad memories. When the opportunity at Saint Basile came up, he arranged for an interview, and when he was offered the job of assistant police chief, he accepted it immediately. He managed to move and get himself settled in Vermont within three weeks of accepting the job offer.

The people in Saint Basile accepted Scott right away. He was congenial and made it a point to get to know as many of the locals as he could. He was a handsome man with an easy going personality, and he quickly earned himself the reputation of being the most eligible yet most unattainable bachelor in the entire lake region. Some of the single women he had dated said that he secretly enjoyed that reputation and that he worked hard to cultivate it. In reality, he was simply not ready for a serious relationship. He had been deeply in love with his wife, and after her death he found it difficult to imagine being attracted to another woman. He had gone out with a few women when he first moved to Saint Basile, but he never quite connected with anyone. He thought that he would eventually like to find that special someone to share dinner or a movie with on a weekend, and now he wondered if Carly Richardson might be that someone.

Scott had an idea that Carly had gone through something very similar, although she didn't seem willing to talk about it. He was very curious about why she left a good job with a prominent law firm in Boston. What had happened to her that had caused her to change her life so dramatically? He found her to be not only very interesting and very attractive but also very mysterious. He intended to find out more about her and solve that mystery.

TEN

The newest owners of Lakeview Farm, Sean and Kate Malone, were in their mid-thirties, and very new to rural living. The locals placed bets among themselves on how long they would last in the frigid Saint Basile winters. Most said they would be out of there before their first year was out. A few thought they might make it, but they were a very small minority.

The Malones had made a decision to move to Vermont after struggling to make ends meet for almost a year in Boston. Sean had gone through a period of severe depression after his business failed, and he spent months in outpatient treatment before he and Kate decided that they needed a complete change in their lives, one that necessitated a move from the expensive Boston area. Both thought that a move to a new environment might be the best thing for them. Kate had summered in Vermont when she was young and had always hoped that she would live there one day with her own family. At her insistence, Sean agreed to the move. Their marriage had been difficult from the beginning. Sean was moody and his behavior was erratic at times. Kate's family despised him and had warned her not to marry him, but she couldn't see beyond his flashy good looks and charming flattery. She first noticed the change in him after their daughter Maura was born. He didn't pay much attention to the baby, but he constantly tried to draw Kate's attention away from her. He was also was insanely jealous and tried to alienate Kate from her friends and family in order to keep all of her attention on him. She was flattered at first, but when his temper would flare while they were with other people, she began to fear what he might do if provoked. She prayed that moving to a new location and a fresh start would change everything.

Finding a place in Vermont that they could afford had not been easy, and they began looking further and further north. They came across Lakeview Farm by sheer accident. It had been put up for a foreclosure by the bank that held the mortgage. Their real estate agent found the foreclosure announcement and urged them to take a look at the property. They fell in love with the place the minute they pulled into the driveway and were able to purchase the place for what was owed on the mortgage. With the proceeds from the sale of their home in Massachusetts as a down payment, they came away from the deal with a very small and very affordable mortgage payment.

The property sat on the outskirts of Saint Basile. Seventeen acres of prime pastureland gradually sloped down to the edge of the lake. Each field was marked off by rough pudding stonewalls, the kind seen all over rural New England. Here and there, some remnants of wooden fence poked through deep brush and tall grass. The farmhouse itself was a white antique structure that had originally started out with four square rooms. Over the years, each new owner added a room here and there until the place lost all sense of logic and good architectural design. A post-and-beam wood frame barn was built about a hundred yards from the house. At one time, it had been a sturdy structure, but when the Malones bought the place, the roof of the barn was missing some shingles, and the building itself was leaning precariously, propped up by four large posts embedded in the ground.

Near the lake's shoreline, there were remnants of an old sawmill, some of it still visible from the top of the slope. The main building was mostly decayed, with much of it missing some wallboard and foundation stone. Lengths of wood rail fencing lay about a large area of the ground in splintered pieces, and decaying wood planks were strewn around the outside of the building in large uneven piles. The sawmill had been abandoned for over twenty years according to some of the neighbors. Most of them had no recollection of it as a working mill at all, but they knew that it was part of the Lakeview Farm real estate.

The main farmhouse and barn had been empty for four years before the Malones bought it, and the farm needed work every place. Sean's construction background made the renovations fairly easy. They remodeled the downstairs area of the house, opening the dining room up so that the family room was an extension of it. Sean worked on the outside while Kate painted the inside rooms and the kitchen cabinets. They had put aside enough money for a good granite countertop, which made the kitchen look brand new. Kate was able to get a job at the Burlington General Hospital, just about twenty minutes away from home, and she found an excellent daycare facility for Maura, who had just turned three. Sean picked up odd jobs doing carpentry work and within a few months he had built enough of a reputation to allow him to start up a small contracting business again.

They started to feel hopeful about their future and that of their daughter, and their marriage seemed to settle into a more peaceful relationship. Sean was more attentive to both Kate and Maura, and they started doing things as a family once again. St. Basile was an active community, and weekends were usually filled with church suppers or family events at the town commons. Kate started to feel as if her prayers had been answered, but her feeling was short-lived. There were subtle things at first, bursts of temper over nothing, or angry moods that would come on suddenly. Kate worried that Sean was slipping into a depression again, although she could find no reason why it might be happening.

ELEVEN

Kate made friends easily in Saint Basile and was soon involved in a local SPCA volunteer program as well as the YMCA children's program in Burlington. Unlike Kate, Sean kept his distance from everyone and soon became known as an oddball. He was always cordial but never really participated in any conversations that the local guys would get into during a lunch hour or after work at the pub.

It bothered Kate that they hadn't made any friends with other couples their age, and she tried to talk with him about it.

"Sean, I would love to invite the Bennetts for dinner some Saturday night. You know, Mike Bennett…he works at the town garage. Judy works with me, and I think you'd like her," she interrupted him while he was watching a basketball game, and his response was abrupt with annoyance.

"I'm not in the mood for entertaining, Katie. And you work all day. It's too much for you, don't you think? Maybe sometime next month."

"You say that every time I ask about having someone to visit, Sean. I don't understand what your problem is with it. It would be nice to just get together with some friends once in a while."

"Kate, I *said* maybe next month. Now drop the subject, okay?"

He turned his back on her and then turned up the volume on the basketball game, discouraging her from saying anymore. This scene repeated itself so often that Kate just gave up asking. As the months rolled on, the Malones became more and more isolated from the community. Kate's only social contacts came from her job and her volunteer work. Sean rarely bothered with anyone outside of his client circle and shunned invitations from neighbors for picnics and cookouts. It didn't take long for the invitations to stop coming entirely.

TWELVE

C arly felt a lot better after talking to Scott about her lack
of confidence, and she decided to drive out to visit the
Malones on the next Saturday morning. She thought about
calling ahead first but decided that she would just take a chance
that they were home.

Saturday morning came, and she loaded Silk into the truck
and headed out to Lakeview Farm around ten in the morning.
The day was mild with a few scattered clouds casting shadows
across the fields. The farm was about a fifteen-minute ride from
the center of town, and Carly noticed that there were very few
farms in that area. This particular section of Saint Basile was
almost completely isolated from the rest of the small community,
and neighbors were isolated from each other.

She arrived at Lakeview Farm after navigating a few tricky
hairpin turns on the narrow road. The front of the house had
been freshly painted, and she could see that some work was being
done on the roof of the old barn. Just behind the barn, a large
draft horse and a small pony were grazing in a fenced area that
extended across a wide expanse of field.

The house windows were all open, and sheer white curtains
fluttered in and out of a few of them, flirting with the morning
breeze. A little girl was sitting cross-legged on a blanket she had
spread on the grass near the side door. Her dolls were arranged
side by side, and Carly could see her talking to them as she
poured each one a cup of imaginary tea. A man, the little girl's
father, Carly suspected, was loading hay into the loft above the
barn door. He turned when he heard the car door slam, and his
eyes locked onto Carly's for an instant. Although the day was
warm, she felt a cold chill pass through her body, and she shivered
a little as she looked back at him. He abruptly turned his back to

her and continued unloading the hay. She thought it odd that he didn't wave or extend any kind of welcome, but she quickly lost the thought when she saw the smiling redheaded woman walking toward her. She let Silk out of the truck, and he sprung off across the open field in front of the barn, returning to sit on the blanket beside the little girl as she welcomed him to her tea party.

Kate Malone was anxious to make friends, and she was genuinely delighted that Carly had stopped by. She had seen Carly in town and had wanted to meet her but never had the chance to introduce herself.

"I am so glad that you stopped to visit, Carly," Kate said as they entered the house.

"I've wanted to meet you. Scott has told me all kinds of nice things about you. It gets kinda lonely way out here. I'm used to the city—Boston, as a matter of fact. And sometimes there is just a little too much peace and quiet up here, if you know what I mean. I'm glad that I have a job a few days a week. Gets me out with people at least.

" I'm happy you were home," Carly said. "Sorry to come by unannounced, but Scott didn't think you would mind. I just took a chance that you would be in this morning."

Kate ushered Carly into the kitchen and poured a cup of coffee for each of them.

"I know exactly what you mean, Kate, about keeping busy," Carly said. "I grew up in the Boston area, too, and I was in the city all the time. I do love it here, but you're right. It does get a bit lonesome."

"What brought you up here, Carly, if you don't mind my asking?"

Carly closed her eyes, trying to decide quickly if she should go into the whole unpleasant story. Instead, she offered a reasonable answer, enough to satisfy the question for the time being.

"I just needed a change. I have a law degree, but I hated working at my father's law firm, and I couldn't find another job that really got me excited until I got a response to my résumé from Jack McIntyre. I've always loved Vermont, and once I saw Saint Basile, I guess I knew that this is where I had to be."

"We came up here for just about the same reasons," Kate told her. "I really think this move has been good for us. I just wish sometimes that there was a little more activity around here. I'm having a hard time getting used to being so far away from everything."

"How does your husband like it here, Kate?" Carly asked.

"I think he's a lot happier than me up here. He seems to enjoy the farm lifestyle, and his business has certainly been better here than it was back home," Kate replied. "I just wish there was more of a social life for me."

"Where are you from originally?" Carly asked.

"Sean was born in South Boston, and I grew up on the South Shore. He had a huge family. Five sisters and three brothers. Typical Irish Catholic. You know, lots of kids, father never home, mother worn out all the time."

Carly laughed at the comment.

"How did you meet him?"

"We were both at a party on the Cape, Falmouth Heights, actually. He came in with a bunch of guys, and I think we just connected, you know? He walked right over to me, and before I knew it we were out on the deck dancing and making out! I remember thinking that he was the most handsome guy I had ever seen."

"I saw man loading hay when I got here. Was that Sean?" Carly asked.

"That was him! He just picked some fresh hay up this morning, and it always takes him a while to get it sorted out and in the barn."

Carly looked at the clock on the kitchen wall and realized that she had been there longer than she had planned. She thought that she ought to leave and not wear out her welcome on the first visit.

"Kate, I have to head back to town. I am so glad we had a chance to meet, and it was wonderful talking with you," she said. "I hope we can get together again real soon."

Just as she stood up to leave, the kitchen door burst open. Silk was outside, barking in a low, almost angry tone, and she wondered what had caught his attention. Sean came into the kitchen, bits of hay still clinging to his flannel shirt and jeans. Carly noticed a flicker of tension pass across Kate's face.

"Sean," Kate said, "I want you to meet Carly Richardson. She's new on the police department and moved up her from the Boston area, just like us."

He stared at Carly for a moment as if he were looking right through her and then looked away before extending his hand, avoiding any further eye contact.

"Pleased to meet you, Carly," he said.

"Same here, Sean. This is a beautiful place you have, and I'm so glad that I got a chance to meet Kate and you."

She kept looking at him. There was something about him, something distantly familiar. *Maybe just a déjà vu moment,* she thought and shrugged it off.

Sean turned away abruptly and headed toward the family room, leaving a trail of hay wisps behind him on the wooden floor. Kate was clearly relieved that he had left the room. Just then, the little girl came in for a drink of water. Kate introduced her to Carly.

"Maura, this is Carly Richardson. And guess what? She is a police officer! What do you think of that?"

Maura edged closer to Carly cautiously and reached out to grab her hand. She was a miniature of her mother, down to the bridge of freckles across her nose.

"Hello, Carly," she said, flashing a bright little smile. "Are you going to come back to visit us, and will you bring your dog back? I like him."

Carly smiled.

"I hope so, Maura. I think Silk liked you too!"

Kate handed Carly her jacket.

"Carly, please don't be a stranger. I'm always home in the afternoon and on the weekends. I would love to get together with you again soon."

"We can make some plans right now, Kate. From what I see in the local newspapers, there's a lot to do around here on the weekends. Why don't we plan go to some of those autumn fairs that are popping up all over the place? I love those things, but I hate to go alone. Why don't we try to go to Saint Basile Harvest Fair that opens in a couple of weeks. What do you say?"

Kate loved the idea. "That's a deal, Carly. We'll talk before that, just to finalize plans."

They hugged, promising to talk in a few days.

Carly headed back to her car, with Silk hard on her heels. She was pleased that she made the trip to Lakeview Farm and was happy that she found a new and interesting friend. She was not quite sure what to think about Sean Malone. He made her uncomfortable, and she sensed that Kate was a little edgy when he came into the kitchen, almost as if she was nervous about having a guest in the house.

As soon as Carly left, Sean stormed back into the kitchen where Kate was cleaning up the dishes.

"What brought *her* out here, Kate? Did you invite her or something?"

Kate turned from the sink to face him, annoyed by his tone. "No, Sean. I didn't invite her. Scott Eames suggested that she stop by and visit. She moved up here from Boston a couple of months ago, and she's lonesome. That's all. And I liked her a lot. We got along real well," Kate replied.

"Well, don't go making a habit of having her here, that's all. I don't like the idea of cops around the place. I don't care how nice they are."

"Sean, you just don't want anybody here, do you? I'm starting to feel like a hermit. If I want her to visit, then by God, I'm going to have her here for a visit. I'm sick of you isolating me from everyone."

Kate was angry. She stood squarely in front of Sean, hands on her hips, eyes flashing.

He reached out and grabbed her by her right arm, squeezing until she cried out in pain from his grip. "You listen to me, Kate, and you listen up real good. If I tell you I don't want someone here, then that's the way it's going to be, girlie. And don't you forget it."

"Sean, let go. You're hurting me," Kate cried.

He squeezed her arm hard once more then released his grip, leaving red imprints where his fingers had been.

Leaving Kate in tears in the kitchen, he returned to the family room to watch the rest of the game. Maura had been in the doorway to the family room the entire time, and Sean had nearly knocked her over as he brushed by her. She moved aside quickly, and after he had passed, she went into the kitchen to her mother.

"Are you okay, Mama? Why are you crying?" the little girl asked. Kate bent down and picked her up.

"I'm okay, honey. I just hit my elbow on something, and it hurt. I'm okay."

Kate didn't want Maura to know that Sean had hurt her, but her arm was starting to bruise up where he had grabbed her. She pulled the sleeve of her sweater down so that Maura couldn't see the marks his fingers had left. Kate put the coffeepot and the dishes in the sink and finished washing them up. Maura dragged a little footstool to Kate's side and stood watching her mother intently. When Kate finished, she gave Maura a kiss on the cheek.

"C'mon, baby girl, let's go upstairs and get you into a bubble bath. Would you like that?"

Maura squealed with delight and ran ahead of Kate through the family room, waiting for her at the foot of the stairs. Sean was watching a soccer game and didn't pay any attention to Maura when she passed him. Kate walked behind his chair, heading to the staircase.

"Hey, Katie. You okay? I didn't mean to grab you so hard."

His voice was cold, without a hint of contrition. He didn't look at her, never taking his eyes from the television screen. Kate didn't acknowledge the apology. She just kept walking silently toward the stairs, stepping as far away from him as she could.

Rachel called Carly that evening, and Carly brought up the subject of her discomfort around Sean again.

"I can't put my finger on it, Rachel," she said. "But the guy gives me the creeps. This was the first time I met him, but I have to tell you, just looking at him gave me the chills. There is just something about him that's not right. Silk was really hostile toward him, which freaked me out too. But I love his wife, and I know you'll like her too."

"Wow, Carly. I have never heard you talk about anyone like this before. You've got pretty good instincts, so if I were you, I'd keep an eye on this guy. Or at least keep a safe distance. Who knows? This guy could be an ax murderer or something," Rachel replied in a joking tone. "Maybe I'll get to meet him when I come up next month!"

"Yeah, I would really love to get your opinion on him. His wife is terrific. You'll love her! I don't know what she sees in him, but she seems to care for him a lot, and who am I to judge? I'll keep you posted. And I can't wait to see you! Don't disappoint me."

"I won't," Rachel promised. "I'll definitely see you in a few weeks. Looks like I can be there the first weekend in November for sure. Maybe I'll get to meet the Malones *and* Scott while I'm there!"

THIRTEEN

C arly made a habit of staying in touch with Kate, and over the next few weeks, they spent much of their free time together; but whenever they planned something, Kate always insisted on meeting Carly in town instead of at the farm.

"No need to have you drive way out here, Carly. It's easier to meet at your place," Kate would tell her. Carly thought it was odd that Kate always insisted on meeting at Carly's place or downtown somewhere, but she didn't argue with her. They went to a few of the local fairs and always made a point to stop at one or two of the antique dealer shops along the sides of the road. Lunch was always on the agenda, and it was often the best part of the day. They found that they could talk for hours about anything and everything. The one thing that Carly never mentioned to Kate was the accident that had killed Rob. It was too painful to discuss, and she didn't think that Kate needed to know about it. Kate prodded her once in a while about her life in Cambridge, and Carly would always make sure that her answers didn't border too close on personal information.

It bothered Carly that Kate was driving into town all the time to meet her, but every time she offered to pick Kate up, there was always an excuse ready about why she shouldn't. After a few times, Carly stopped asking, beginning to suspect that Sean had something to do with Kate's excuses.

There were a couple of occasions when Carly was just driving by the farm on a work patrol and decided to stop in to see Kate. Sean was always noticeably absent from the house during these visits although Carly sensed he was on the premises, watching to see when she would leave. Kate didn't talk about him much, which

Carly found strange, but she held back from asking Kate about him, sensing that Sean was not a subject Kate wanted to discuss.

Sean was the exact opposite from Kate, and Carly often wondered what Kate saw in him. He was sullen, rarely smiled, and talked very little. She frequently caught glimpses of him when she visited, but he seemed to work hard at avoiding any contact with her. There were times when she could feel him staring at her even though she couldn't see him. On the few occasions that she actually came in contact with him, he rudely ignored her presence, and always, lying just beneath the surface, was her overwhelming sense that she had met him someplace in her past. She was often tempted to ask him if they had met when they were all in Massachusetts, but she didn't seem to find the right time to raise the question. On one of her drop-by visits, Carly asked Kate if Sean disliked her.

"Oh, of course he likes you, Carly. Don't be silly," Kate said.

"He's shy, that's all. Never was comfortable around girls anyway, so he won't talk much."

"I would have thought that he would be very comfortable around girls, having grown up with five sisters," Carly commented.

"He didn't really have a close-knit family, and I think being the youngest, he was left to fend for himself a lot," Kate replied. "His brothers were long gone from the house by the time he was in junior high school. I don't know his sisters very well, but I suspect they were all working their own agendas and didn't spend much time with him. We have absolutely no contact with any of them and have no idea where his father is these days. I know for a fact that his mother was an alcoholic. She was dead by the time she was fifty. Sean told me that he and one of his sisters found her dead on the bathroom floor with an empty bottle of gin in her hand. Sean said she used to be drunk every night by the time the younger kids were all in bed, and he didn't get much attention from her at all. One of his older sisters actually raised him."

Carly knew there was more to this guy than what Kate was sharing. She heard around town that Sean was getting a reputation for being antisocial. He stopped at the pub once in a while for a beer or two after work, and the guys who hung out at the bar told her they thought he was pleasant enough—"just a quiet sort who likes to mind his own business and not go poking into anyone else's." Carly saw him there on occasion when she was making her rounds, sitting alone at the bar, never joining any of the dart games or table conversations that were always underway. She tried to make conversation with him but could never get him to say more than a few words about anything. She also found it odd that he would never look directly at her. Whenever she spoke to him, he always looked down at his shoes, obviously avoiding any eye contact with her.

Silk didn't like Sean at all. The dog was always tense when Sean was around, holding his ears flat against his head, never taking his eyes off the man. Sean tried to pat him a few times, but Silk always pulled away and leaned close to Carly's legs as if trying to protect her. Carly knew that dogs can sense when something is wrong about a person, and her own feelings about Sean Malone were heightened by the dog's protective behavior.

She brought the subject up with Scott, curious to see what he might think about the situation.

"I can't get rid of this uncomfortable feeling when Sean Malone is around me," she told Scott. "I don't know what it is. Even Silk is uneasy around him. He slinks around with his tail between his legs and won't leave my side at all. Growls sometimes too. You know that's out of character for this good old dog."

She leaned down and gave Silk a behind-the-ears scratch.

"I agree with you about the dog, Carly," Scott said. "But maybe you're just letting your imagination run away with you, or maybe your cop training has gone to your head. Maybe you should check America's most wanted!"

"Come on, Scott. Be serious. I just happen to think this guy is a creep!"

"Has he said anything or done anything to make you feel like this?" Scott asked.

"No, not really. He is obviously careful about not making eye contact with me, and when I visit sometimes, I always feel as if he's just lurking about, listening to everything we say. And I notice Kate is always on edge when he is around too. It's like she is worried that he will say or do something out of line. Ah, you're probably right. Just my imagination."

"I wouldn't worry too much about it. Tell you what. I'll keep my ears open and promise I will let you know if I hear anything. Okay?"

Scott gave her a hug, holding on to her just a bit longer than a comfort hug would call for, and headed out to make his rounds. To Carly's surprise, the hug felt very nice. It was the first time she had felt that way since losing Rob. It started her wondering if she had finally started to put the grieving process aside.

FOURTEEN

The town of Saint Basile was no stranger to frigid winters and abundant snowfalls, but in early November, there were signs that the coming winter would be record-breaking by all accounts. The old-timers commented that the squirrels were sporting thicker coats than usual and that some of the hibernating animals had disappeared far too early.

The first snowstorm hit the area on November 5, dumping several inches of heavy wet snow and then freezing everything solid with subzero temperatures. Carly was totally surprised by the early turn of the weather.

"Is this weather the norm for early November up here?" she asked Scott. "I expected some heavy stuff this winter, but not this early."

"Not totally unusual," he said. "But this one is earlier and heavier than what we've had in past years. I'm a bit surprised myself. Mother Nature must be letting us know about things to come. Last time I saw this was about eight years ago, and that winter was a real ballbuster. Even the lake froze early that year."

Carly grimaced at the prospect of being iced in all winter.

"Well, I hope this one clears up fast. My friend Rachel is coming to visit this weekend. I would hate to see her get stuck in a bad storm."

It took two days for the storm to move out totally and make its way to the Canadian Maritimes. The roads were a mess, and the air was damp with a constant raw wind blowing off the lake. Carly reluctantly decided to call Rachel and have her postpone her visit to another time. Rachel had been following the weather reports and was thinking along those same lines.

"I was going to call you tonight about coming another time," she told Carly. "It wouldn't be much fun if we couldn't get out and about a little, and it sounds like that won't happen this weekend."

"Yeah, I think you're right, Rachel. As much as I was looking forward to seeing you, I don't want to drag you up here in this weather. Can we plan for something just before Christmas?" Carly asked.

"Absolutely. I'll check my travel schedule and get back to you in a couple of days, okay? You be careful driving in that stuff."

Rachel promised again to call her, and Carly, disappointed that her friend wouldn't be coming, was also relieved that she wouldn't worry about her making a long trip in bad weather. With Rachel's trip postponed, Carly found herself with a huge hole in her weekend.

She spent a peaceful Saturday watching a few rented movies and catching up on some reading. But the night was not as restful. Her worries about the weather brought old anxieties to the surface with paralyzing intensity. She was in and out of vivid dreams about the accident all through Saturday night, and by Sunday morning, she was totally exhausted. She had to get out of the condo for a while, and she decided to head into town and grab some breakfast at the diner. The roads had been plowed again the night before, and most areas were down to bare pavement. She had Silk with her and thought she might just walk him around the town common after breakfast, thinking that some exercise might get rid of her stress.

She parked in front of the diner, leaving Silk in the car with the windows opened a crack.

Scott was at the counter having breakfast, and he spotted Carly the minute she walked in.

"Hey, you," he called out. "What the heck are you doing in town this morning? I thought you had company this weekend." He motioned for her to join him. "Come, sit here beside me," he said, patting the empty stool to his right.

She walked over to the counter, happy to see him.

"This is a nice surprise," she answered. "I didn't expect to find you here this morning either! I think I was getting cabin fever. Rachel and I agreed to cancel out on her trip this weekend because of the weather reports. I didn't want her to get stuck up here. So…here I am, wandering around by myself!"

"Well then, we can have breakfast together. What are you doing later?" Scott asked.

"I thought I would just take Silk for a walk around town. We both need the exercise, and it's not a bad day," she told him.

"Would you like some company? I'm not doing anything at all this morning. Don't have to be at the department until two. What do you say?" he asked.

"I'd love some company! I bet Silk would like to have you join up too. Much more fun having two humans to play with," she said.

They finished breakfast and headed out of the diner to get Silk and then walked toward the town common. It was several blocks away, and they chatted as they walked along Main Street.

"So, Carly, what's got you so uptight that you need to walk a few miles this morning?" Scott asked.

She didn't want to go into any detail with him about the accident and the recurrent dreams she had, so she blamed everything on the snow.

"It's just the weather, I think, Scott. I'm not used to being snowed in all the time. I think it just makes me restless. That's all. I've always loved snow, but I don't remember ever seeing this much accumulation in such a short time. My dad used to take me skiing a lot when I was a kid, and I thought the snow was fabulous back then. The more the better, especially on the slopes. Guess my perspective has changed! Now I am starting to dread the stuff."

He seemed satisfied with her answer and didn't press her any further. It took about ten minutes to reach the commons, and once they were there, Carly let Silk off the leash so he could run around for a while. He immediately took off after a squirrel, sending it scurrying up one of the large pine trees. The squirrel chattered angrily at the barking dog below it, keeping it interested in staying at the foot of the tree while the squirrel climbed into the higher branches.

Carly and Scott found a bench near the frozen frog pond and cleared the snow from it so that they could sit down and enjoy the warmth of the sun and the clear day. Their rest didn't last long because Silk got tired of barking at the squirrel, who by that time had hopped to another tree. He ran to where Carly and Scott were sitting, pestering to continue the walk.

"I guess he's trying to tell us something," Carly said. "We probably ought to start heading back anyway. You still have to change and get to work in a little while."

"Okay with me," Scott said. "Want to grab a coffee on the way back?"

"Sure. I think the diner is still open," Carly replied.

With the dog prancing along between them, they headed back along Main Street, stopping to get two coffees to go just as the diner was putting up its Closed sign in the window.

Scott walked her back to her car before he headed down the street to the department building.

"Thanks for the company too, Scott. It was nice spending some off-duty time with you!"

"You're very welcome," he said. "We should do this more often. At least it gives Silk a chance to run around and get some exercise!"

Carly agreed, thinking that Silk wouldn't be the only one getting some benefit.

FIFTEEN

After that storm, the sky was almost always steel gray and filled with billowing, moisture-laden clouds. Snow fell just about every day, sometimes in flurries, sometimes in stinging squalls of crystallized flakes. The lake had started to freeze around the shore edges, and the small streams and brooks had been channeled into thin rivulets by the ice. There were days when the streets were impassable and slick with ice.

Most of Carly's time was spent checking on families who lived on the outskirts of the town to make sure that they had heat and enough food. Scott had to engage the "call" officers to help because there was more workload than he and Carly could handle. Jack McIntyre was hardly available, so the burden fell on Scott and Carly to coordinate everything. The run of bad weather made it seem more like late January than early November, and Carly worried about what the rest of the winter would be like. She stayed in touch with Kate by phone but had not had time to visit. Even her off days were duty filled because of the weather.

The police department had a four-wheel drive truck, which became Carly's main mode of transportation. By the time she got home at night, she was exhausted from the sheer effort of maneuvering the truck on icy, snow-furrowed streets and unplowed driveways. The constant snowfall had begun to take a toll on her, and she was restless at night, waking every few hours and obsessively checking the weather. Silk was showing signs of anxiety, not wanting to go out unless Carly went with him. She felt guilty about the dog because she knew her own restlessness was transferring over to him. When he was outside, his hackles were always raised along the ridge of his neck, and his head was held high as he paced back and forth with his nose to the wind.

He pulled at his leash when she walked him as if he were trying to break away from her and chase some invisible intruder away. When he was with her in the office, he lay in front of the main door, whining, until either Carly or Scott pulled him away and sent him to his bed by the woodstove. Scott was beginning to get annoyed with him.

"What the hell is wrong with that dog, Carly? He's never acted like this. It's driving me nuts. You'll have to leave him home if he doesn't stop."

"I don't know what's got into him, Scott. He's turned into a bundle of nerves lately. Must be the weather. I'll call the vet if he keeps it up much longer. Something serious might be wrong with him," she replied. She made an effort to stay calm herself, and when she did, Silk settled down immediately.

Rachel finally made the trip to Saint Basile in mid-November. There was still a heavy snow cover on the entire town, but she and Carly managed to get to Burlington for a full day of shopping, ending up in one of the local bistros for an early dinner. On the way back to Saint Basile, Rachel asked Carly about the Malones.

"You haven't said much about your friend Kate, Carly. Are you still visiting her as much as you were?" she asked.

"I haven't seen her all that much in a couple of weeks," Carly replied.

"This weather has kept me and Scott out straight, just trying to check on people. Especially the ones on the outskirts of town. I've talked with Kate a couple of times, but that's about it."

"You thought something was wrong at their place when I talked to you last. What do you think is going on?"

"Honestly, Rachel, I don't know. But there is definitely a problem. If I were a betting girl, I'd lay a wager that that husband of hers is abusive. I really can't do anything except keep a watch on her, I guess."

Rachel stared out the truck window for a minute, thinking.

"What about the little girl, Carly? Do you think she is okay?"

"Right now, I think so. I haven't noticed anything out of the ordinary with her. But if he is abusive to Kate, it's a matter of time before he starts on Maura. The guy just gives me the creeps."

They spent the rest of the evening at the condo. Carly opened a bottle of wine and fixed a platter of sandwiches. They talked for hours about Carly's job, Rachel's job, Carly's parents, and finally Rachel asked the question she had been holding back all day.

"So, Carly, any good-looking guys up here? Anyone caught your pretty green eyes yet?" Rachel noticed that Carly was blushing.

"Not really, but…"

"C'mon, Carly, spill it!" Rachel said.

"Well, Scott Eames is a pretty nice guy. We get along really well, and I have a feeling that he is a little interested."

"Yeah? And what about you?"

Carly blushed again. "I have to admit, I've wondered what it would be like to just go out with him, you know. Just a movie or something, but then I start thinking this is way too soon and start feeling guilty and everything. Probably stupid at this point, but I can't help it."

"Have you told him anything about Rob or about what happened?" Rachel asked.

"No, but I've thought about it. Just haven't had the right moment to bring it up, I guess. And he hasn't asked about my background at all, so I haven't felt pressured to say anything."

"He sounds like a really nice guy, Carly, and if he asks you out, you had better go. I'll be really upset with you if you don't!" Rachel said.

"Well, it's unlikely that it will ever happen, but if it does, you'll be the first to know."

"Any chance I can get to meet him this weekend? Or Kate?"

"I thought we might take a ride out to Lakeview Farm in the morning if the weather is still good and then catch up with Scott when we get back. I would really like to get your take on Sean too if he's around."

They went to bed around midnight and woke up to the promise of yet another snowstorm brewing. Carly fixed a big breakfast for them, and when the news stations kept breaking in to regular programming with storm alerts, they both thought that Rachel had better get an early start home before the weather turned ugly. She called Kate and cancelled the visit and then let Scott know that Rachel would be leaving by noon and would have to meet him another time. Rachel left just as the first flakes were beginning to drift to the ground. Carly turned to the weather channel for a storm update. As soon as Rachel pulled out of the parking lot, Carly cringed when she heard the report for northern Vermont—another four to six inches of snow forecast for Sunday and Sunday night.

Carly had always looked forward to winter snowstorms. Some of her favorite childhood memories were of the vacation ski trips to Vermont with her father. Hannah never joined them on these excursions, and Carly relished the time alone with her dad. They would ski for hours, no matter what the weather was like. Sometimes snow fell on them the entire time they were on the slopes, freezing their hair and eyelashes with coats of white frost. Carly loved the feel of the cold white flakes on her face, the smell of it in the air, and beauty of it on the distant mountains. But this weather was different from anything she had ever seen. There was something sinister about this weather, something purposeful and calculating. She sometimes felt as if the snow itself had taken on a kind of vengeful persona, determined to wreak havoc on the little town by trapping it in an icy embrace.

She was cold all the time, even when the heat was turned up high in her condo. She went to bed with layers of clothing, heavy socks, and a mountain of down comforters, and still, she could not seem to get warm. The cold seized her entirely, and she began to fear that she was ill. She was unable to sleep for more than a few hours at a stretch, waking continually to check the weather from her bedroom window. Obsessed with the snow, she thought of nothing else when she was alone. Silk was troubled, too, and paced all night long, his nails clicking rhythmically across the bare wooden floor of the bedroom. She finally admitted to herself that she was letting the weather get the best of her, blaming herself for Silk's unease because he sensed that she was on edge. She knew that some of her anxiety was residue from the accident that killed Rob. Each time there was a snowfall, the memory of that evening flooded her mind. The sound of the plow, the faceless man, and the memory of Rob lifeless on the road consumed her. She tried to convince herself that what was happening in Vermont was just normal northern weather. But every time the sky darkened, the anxieties welled up in her, and she couldn't shake them off no matter how hard she tried.

Scott couldn't help but notice the subtle change in her and worried that something was seriously wrong. He asked her several times if she was all right, but she just shrugged the question off, making excuses that she was up late or that the dog kept her awake the night before. He knew she was being evasive, but he didn't push at her any further.

"Just want you to know that I am a good listener, Carly. That is if you feel like talking," he told her.

"Really, Scott. I'm okay. Just tired. I promise I'll let you know if something is really going on," she replied.

She would have liked nothing better than to talk to Scott about her concerns. She trusted him but was reluctant to unload her problems onto him.

When Rachel called her that evening, she could tell from the sound of Carly's voice that something was bothering her.

"Carly, what's going on? You sound terrible, so don't try to fluff this off. I haven't heard you sound like this since the accident. What is it? Tell me?"

Carly hesitated, but her friend was persistent, and she knew that Rachel wouldn't let up on her until she answered.

"I'm okay, Rachel, really, I am. Just dead tired and frustrated by this stormy weather. I'm so sick of this constant snow I could scream. It's never ending. Every single day, more snow. I'm starting to have second thoughts about coming up here."

"Are you still having those bad dreams?" Rachel asked.

"Oh yeah. Almost every night. And if I'm not startled out of a sound sleep by a nightmare, then I'm up all night checking the weather. I'm driving myself and Silk crazy."

"Carly, do you want me to come up there for a few days?"

"No, Rach, I'll be fine. Just keep in touch, okay?" Rachel had to end the call in order to get to a morning meeting.

"I'll check back with you in a couple of days, Carly. But if you need to talk, just pick up the phone and call. I don't care what time it is, okay?"

"I will. Thanks. You're always there for me, and I appreciate it."

Carly thought about calling Scott just to talk. He had said he was a good listener. She started to dial his number then stopped and hung up the phone. She was afraid that if she really unloaded on him, he would steer as clear away from her as he possibly could. She didn't want to take that chance.

SIXTEEN

After Rachel left, there was a little break in the weather and the Saturday before Thanksgiving, Carly got herself up and dressed early, fixed herself and Silk some breakfast, and headed out to visit with Kate. She hadn't seen her for a couple of weeks and thought to herself, *Kate Malone is just what I need.*

She didn't call first to see if Kate was home.

It had snowed the night before, and a couple of inches of fresh powder lay over the town like a new fleece blanket. The roads were cleared, and the sun was shining by the time she got going. She felt uplifted for the first time in weeks and hummed to herself as she drove toward the outskirts of town. She passed by acres of glittering white pastureland that stretched out on either side of the narrow country road. Dripping icicles hung from snow-laden tree branches, turning pieces of the morning sunlight into rainbows of color. Even Silk was relaxed, wagging his tail while Carly sang Christmas carols to him.

It was around ten thirty when she finally reached the long driveway that led to the Malones' house. The driveway had been cleared, and it looked like the walkways had been shoveled out. She noticed a couple of crows sitting on the fence alongside the driveway, bickering with each other over a scrap of food. Three more crows were perched in the branches of the oak tree in front of the house. She had seen crows around that property before, but never so close to the house. Silk spotted the birds and jumped from the front of the truck cab to the back with excitement. He was anxious to jump out of the truck and give the squawking birds a good chase. Carly could see some movement in the fenced area behind the barn and thought that Sean had probably put the animals out for some fresh air. There were a couple of goats, a huge Belgian draft horse named Rocky, and a little Welsh pony named Daisy. Three acres behind the barn were fenced in for the animals, and a small arena had been made so that Maura would have a safe place to ride Daisy when the weather was good.

Carly saw Sean leaving the barn just as she was getting out of the truck. Silk was barking furiously now to get out, and when she opened the door, he bounded off through the deep snow, chasing the quarreling yellow-eyed crows from the fence.

She got out of the truck and called to Sean. "Sean…hey," she yelled. "How are you? I haven't seen you in ages."

He stopped and stared at her for a minute as if she were a stranger then walked toward her, carrying a feed bucket. He didn't return the greeting and just kept walking straight at her. She shrugged off the uneasy feeling she always got when he was around her and gave him a broad smile as he got closer.

He stopped a few feet in front of her, pulling his cap over his eyes so that his face was partially hidden from view.

"Stopping to see Kate?" he asked.

"Just for an hour or so," Carly said. "How are things going, Sean? Are you keeping busy?"

He lifted his cap a bit, his eyes narrowed to small slits as he answered her. "Well, if you really want to know, things pretty much stink! My contract jobs have just about stopped because of this stormy weather," he said. "Good thing Kate's working. It's pretty tough making ends meet these days."

He was tense, like a coiled wire ready to spring open. Not wanting to irritate him further, Carly chose her next words carefully, trying to sound upbeat. "Don't worry, Sean. I think things will break soon," she said, trying to sound cheerful. "Gotta think positive. At least we'll have a white Christmas, and maybe we'll get that famous January thaw this year."

Sean stood in front of her for a minute more, and without answering, he pulled his cap back down over his eyes and then abruptly turned away and headed toward the barn.

Without looking back at her, he shouted, "Kate's in the kitchen. Just go on in."

She watched him trudge back toward the open barn door, thinking that his behavior was beyond strange, even for him, but she soon displaced the thought when she saw Kate at the kitchen door.

"Carly! What a wonderful surprise! Why didn't you call? I would have fixed us something fancy for lunch," Kate squealed.

Specks of white flour dotted her arms, and she wiped her hands quickly on her apron before giving Carly a strong hug and pushing her into the cushioned chair at the kitchen table.

"Sit, sit, sit," she said.

"I have a fresh pot of coffee on, and Maura is upstairs making a tent in her room. I'm dying to hear what's been going on in town."

Carly sat back, enjoying the warmth coming from the old cast-iron stove. While Kate was busy bustling about getting coffee mugs and muffins on the table, Carly started to bring her up-to-date on all the latest gossip.

While she was talking, Carly noticed several large bruises on Kate's right arm. Her eyes widened, and she stopped in midsentence, staring at the dark purple marks above Kate's elbow.

"What happened to your arm, Kate? You have a couple of nasty bruises there."

Kate hesitated before she answered, "Oh, the bruises? Oh, I um…I was lifting a hay bale, and the strap just sort of sunk into my arm. Left a couple of beauties, didn't they?" Kate's tone was nonchalant. Carly looked at the bruises more closely, certain that they were not caused by any hay bale strap. The more she studied them, the more she realized that they were impressions left by fingers pressing into the fleshy part of Kate's upper arm. Carly knew that Kate was lying about what happened, but she didn't press her any further at the moment. Tears welled up in Kate's eyes, and she tugged at the sleeve of her sweater to pull it down, trying unsuccessfully to hide the black-and-blue marks.

Carly spotted an opportunity to get Kate to talk, and she jumped on it. "C'mon, Katie. Talk to me, girl. No good to hold it in," she said. Kate got up and looked out the door as if to see if Sean was still in the barn. When she didn't see him outside, she sat down again and began to tell Carly how things really were. The smiling young woman who greeted Carly just minutes ago was gone.

"Sean has just about closed the business, Carly. Just before the third snowstorm, things just came to a halt, and he just stopped trying to get work. And he's sullen and bad tempered almost all the time these days. He goes into Burlington a lot, too, and he never used to do that. Hangs out at a place called the Magic Hat Brewery, or so he tells me, and he comes home drunk when he's been there. He keeps bringing home these stupid bottle caps with sayings on them and glues them to the wall in the family room. And he has this stupid T-shirt that he wears every single day, like a uniform or something with "Life Is Crap, No Beer" written on the front of it. He's always cross with Maura, and she gets so hurt when he yells at her over nothing mostly. He spanked her the other day, hard, because she broke one of his sports trophies. He's never hit her before, Carly. I'm so worried, and I don't know what to do. I'm working a few days a week, and I am nervous about leaving Maura home with him. I know it must be hard for him to be out of work, but he's changing. He's just not the same, and I'm scared."

Carly knew for certain now that her intuition about Sean had been right. He had been physically abusive to Kate, and she could see and hear the evidence right in front of her.

"What are you afraid of, Kate? Are you afraid that Sean will hurt Maura or you?"

"I don't know, Carly. He just scares me lately, that's all. I don't think he would hurt us on purpose, but he gets into these rages, and I never know what's going to happen."

"Kate, has he always had a temper like this?"

"I think he used to get in a lot of trouble when he was a kid. His sister told me that he was in fights all the time, and I know he spent some time in juvenile detention when he was sixteen. But when I met him, he was always a perfect gentleman. I honestly never saw him lose his temper, at least not with me. And never with Maura. Now, I feel like I am walking on eggshells all the time so I won't get him going."

Kate started to cry, and Carly leaned over and hugged her. She didn't know what else to do. She wanted to ask Kate if Sean gave her those bruises, but she already knew the answer. Kate would try to protect him, and Carly knew that she wouldn't get a straight answer from her.

There was a noise outside, and Kate jumped up to look out the kitchen door. Silk was barking to come in, and Carly could hear the crunch of Sean's boots as he came up the walkway. She grabbed a towel from the counter, giving it to Kate so she could dry her eyes. Kate scrambled to compose herself before Sean walked in the door. The wind had picked up, and a light cloud of snow flew into the kitchen when the door was opened. Sean came in with the dog right behind him. He never acknowledged Carly's presence, keeping his back to her while he took his jacket and boots off and walked over to the sink to wash up. Silk stood at the door and shook the powdery snow from his coat, spraying cold droplets all around him. Carly noticed Sean's T-shirt, just as Kate had described.

Pretty fitting for the mood he's in right now, she thought.

"Do you want coffee, honey?" Kate asked, trying to keep her voice from quivering.

"Nah," he replied sullenly.

Silk had his tail between his legs, and he moved cautiously to the rear of the kitchen, as far from Sean as he could manage.

"I'm gonna grab a beer and watch the football game for a while. Keep Maura quiet while the game is on, would you please? She's a pain in the neck when I'm trying to watch something."

Still ignoring Carly, he finished drying his hands and headed into the family room, which was just off the kitchen. She waited until he was in his recliner before she got up to put on her jacket. She had the feeling that her visit was fueling Sean's sullen mood, and she decided to leave before things escalated. She leaned close to Kate's ear so that Sean wouldn't hear her.

"Kate, I'm worried sick about you. I get the feeling that Sean is upset that I'm here, so I'll get going, but if you need me for anything at anytime just pick up that phone and call me, okay?"

Kate nodded and helped Carly with her coat.

"I am glad you stopped by, Carly, and I will call, I promise. It's just a bad time right now, I guess," Kate said.

Carly nudged the dog gently from under the table. "C'mon, Silk. We have to go now. Go to the truck." She gave Kate a quick hug and kiss and headed out to the driveway, turning around for one last glimpse at the house before she got in the truck.

As soon as Carly was out the door, Sean stomped back into the kitchen. Kate could tell he was angry. She sat down, pretending to finish her coffee. He pulled out the end chair and sat down, slamming his fist on the table.

"Kate, I thought I told you I didn't want her out here. What did you do, just go and invite her again? You never listen to anything, do you?"

"She just stopped by, Sean, for goodness' sake. What was I supposed to do, tell her to go away? I don't understand why you don't like her. What in the world did she ever do to you?"

He gave her a cold look. "She's a cop. That's enough! And I don't trust her. She's nosy. Next time you want her here, you'd better check with me first, Kate, or I'll throw her out myself!" He got up and went back into the family room, leaving Kate stunned by his outburst.

By the time Carly was on the road heading back to town, the sun had disappeared entirely. She gathered her scarf up tightly around her neck, suddenly feeling ice cold inside, the way she did at night sometimes. The outside temperature was still in the forties, not cold enough to chill her like that. She looked up at the gathering gray clouds moving in quickly from the west. The afternoon had turned gray like the sky, and the dank smell of coming snow filled her nostrils. She was torn about leaving Kate but reminded herself that what happened between Kate and Sean Malone was really not her business. At least not just then.

That night, Carly was more restless than usual. She had trouble falling asleep but finally drifted off after tossing and turning for a couple of hours.

The nightmare gripped her again.

She wandered into a bitter snowstorm, whirling around the tree trunks, driven by biting gusts of wind. The house was barely visible behind the veil of white.

She pushed against the wind and stinging flakes, trying to get up the driveway. The lights were on in the kitchen window, and she could see smoke coming from the chimney at that end of the house. But she couldn't move forward. Each step forced her into deeper snow until the frozen white powder was hugging her from the waist down. She tried to plow herself through, but she was immobilized by the cold embrace of the snow. Her eyes were stinging, and frost was forming on her hair and eyelashes. She called out, but her voice was lost in the wind. She stood frozen in place, screaming into the storm, calling Kate's name. Two crows, their black feathers ruffling in the wind, clung to the fence in front of her, their yellow eyes watching her every move.

Another crow joined them, bobbing its black head and snapping its sharp beak at her when she tried to move. A dog was howling from somewhere behind her, but she couldn't turn to see where it was. She was walled in on all sides by rising snowdrifts. The crows left the fence and circled over her head before they flew toward the house.

She woke up shivering, her heart pounding wildly. It was nearly five in the morning, and she could see large snowflakes tumbling past her bedroom window, tinted by the first streaks of daybreak. The memory of the nightmare was vivid. Her pillow was damp from perspiration, and the bed linens were rumpled into a pile at the foot of the bed. She sat up slowly, feeling with her feet for the fuzzy slippers that she kept beside the bed. Silk was scratching and whining at the bedroom door to be let out. The house was warm enough, but she was freezing cold. Still shivering, she got up, grabbed her fleece robe from the chair, and walked to the window.

The storm looked as if it was winding down, leaving close to two feet of fresh snow on the ground as its parting gift. She made her way to the kitchen, wrapping the heavy robe tightly around her. Through the kitchen window, she watched daylight easing its way up the horizon in bright red and yellow streaks before it disappeared into the heavy gray clouds. She let Silk out, but he just stood at the door whimpering, tail between his legs and ears flat against his head.

"What's wrong, boy? What do you see out there?"

The dog stood motionless, nose to the wind, looking out through the dwindling flurries of snow. Carly put her boots and jacket on and grabbed him by the collar, gently leading him to the bottom of the steps.

"C'mon, Silk, I know you have to pee. It's okay. There's nothing out here."

He finally walked away from her, marked the nearest tree, and then rushed back through the snow to her side, tail still between his legs. She looked out across the field. Nothing was moving except for a few whirls of snow blown about by small wind gusts. She gave him a reassuring pat on the head and turned to go back inside to get ready for work. Before she went in, she stopped and gave one last glance at the frozen white field before closing the door.

Carly finished her breakfast, all the while thinking of Kate Malone and finally making a mental note to call her later in the morning. Kate was in trouble, and Carly knew she had to help her. She wasn't sure what to do, but she knew that she couldn't leave this alone. She was going to dissect this situation until she figured out how to get Kate out of a terrible situation. Rob always called her a picker.

"The trouble with you, Carly, is that you just have to pull that hanging thread from the sweater or pick up the piece of lint from the floor and examine it, don't you? One of these days you're going to pick at the wrong thread and unravel the whole damn sweater, and then you won't be able to put it back together again."

She knew this was the one thing that really annoyed Rob about her. He was right, but she kept picking anyway until she found a solution to whatever problem was at hand. She knew that she was going to pick at the threads dangling at the Malone household and feared that she might unravel things beyond repair.

By five thirty, the maintenance company had finally plowed out the condo parking lots, and the streets appeared to be passable, so she headed for the truck, already a little late for work. By the time she reached the department building, all the main roads had been cleared. Scott arrived at about the same time, and together they made their way to the front door, kicking snow off the stairs on the way. Silk ran ahead and then sat patiently at the door, waiting to get to the warmth from the woodstove.

The building was frigid, and their warm breath ballooned in front of them in puffs of white vapor.

"Scott, would you mind stoking up the woodstove? It's freezing in here," Carly asked.

"Sure, Carly. No problem. I'll get some wood from the shed."

He looked at her, noticing the dark circles under her eyes.

"You okay this morning, Carly?"

"Yeah, I'm fine. Had a real bad dream last night and didn't sleep well."

Scott had an urge to give her a hug, make it better, but knew that would be out of line. Instead, he grabbed the woodbox and headed out the back door while Carly plugged the coffeepot in to make a fresh brew.

Once the stove got going, the room heated up quickly. They each grabbed a mug of coffee and sat at the reception desk, watching the plows finish the cleanup on Main Street for the church crowd.

"Scott, I need to ask your opinion about something. I was at the Malones yesterday, and I am worried about Kate. Sean, too, I guess. Something is wrong out there. The whole atmosphere in the house was tense and uncomfortable, and I thought that Kate seemed, well, anxious around Sean. Have you heard any gossip in town at all?"

She stopped short of telling Scott about the bruises on Kate's arm or that she suspected Sean has been physically abusive to Kate and maybe Maura as well. She wanted to be absolutely sure on those details before she made a public accusation.

Scott listened attentively. "Geez, Carly. I haven't heard anything. But I did run into Sean one day last week, and I thought he looked worn out. He didn't seem to want to talk to me, more or less ignored me," Scott said. "I thought that was kinda funny. Usually, he will chat for a bit, maybe share a joke or two."

"He was downright strange with me yesterday, too," Carly remarked. "I've always thought he didn't like me very much. Maybe jealous because Kate and I get along so well. But he was different yesterday. Detached is the best way I can describe him. He *never* looks me in the eye directly, and I hate it when people do that! I have a funny feeling about him, Scott. Like I have met him before or something. Isn't that weird? Can't quite put my finger on it, but I think he senses something with me as well. And Silk is very wary around him, which is strange. This dog loves everyone he sees. I didn't see Maura either the other day, and she is usually all over me when I visit. Kate said she was upstairs, but I thought it was odd that she didn't come down when she heard that I was there."

Surprised that Carly had opened up a little, Scott offered to see what he could find out. "I'll ask around, Carly," he said. "Tommy Riley might know something. Sean stops in there once in a while."

"I'd really appreciate that, Scott. I'm going to call Kate tomorrow anyway. Just to check."

Carly finished her coffee and headed for the front door with Silk at her side. "I'm going to drive around for a while and check on the roads. Might run by a few of the houses outside of town just to see if they are all right. Be back in a couple of hours."

"Okay, Carly. Just check in with me and let me know where you are," Scott said.

"And by the way, there's a ham and bean supper at the Grange Hall tonight. I'd love to have you come with me if you aren't doing anything. Phil is on call tonight, so we don't have to worry about this place."

Carly stared at him for what he thought was an eternity. Then, she said, "You know what…I would love to go with you. Pick me up at my place around five thirty."

She surprised herself that she agreed, and Scott surprised himself that he had the courage to ask. She smiled at the thought of looking forward to a ham and bean supper, a far cry from the theater dates and concerts that she and Rob used to attend every weekend, but maybe a much-needed change.

Carly wanted Rachel to know what had happened and called her from her cell phone.

Rachel picked up right away.

"Guess what, Rachel! He asked me out!" Carly blurted. "Don't you dare laugh, but we are going to a ham and bean supper at the Grange Hall tonight!" Carly could hear Rachel stifling a giggle, but she replied without hesitating.

"That's terrific, Carly. I'm so glad to hear that you're going out. It will do you good, and who knows where this might go," Rachel replied.

Carly started to laugh herself.

"Oh yes, this is most definitely going to be the highlight of my winter social season. I can tell. But…don't go making more out of this than it is, please! It's just a ham and bean supper!"

"Okay, okay," Rachel said. "But you absolutely have to tell me everything! And just to make sure that you do, I am going to call you tomorrow night."

"All right, Ms. Nosy. I'll talk to you then. Gotta go now. I'm taking a ride out to check on some people. Talk to you later."

The morning was gray, but the snow had decreased to a few flurries. Carly headed up Main Street around ten o'clock, planning to drive by a few of the farms and in particular the Malone farm while she was out. She called Kate on her cell phone but got the voice mail message. She made her way out of town, weaving the truck in and out of the deep ruts in the road. The plows had only made one pass on the side streets, and the going was rough even with a four-wheel drive vehicle. Some people were out shoveling driveways and sidewalks, and as she got further outside of town center, she started seeing tractors moving around the farm properties, plowing snow so that the animals could get outside. It took about a half an hour to reach the Malone place. She wasn't planning to stop, just to drive by and check.

A few lights were on in the house, but none of the walkways had been cleared, and the long gravel drive was still covered with fresh snow. The plows had moved the road snow into several massive drifts at the end of the driveway, nearly blocking the entrance. Snow had been plowed onto those mounds for weeks until their height reached ten feet in some places, hiding some of the property from view. The barn door was closed, and it didn't look like any of the animals were out. She tried Kate's cell phone again, but still got the voice message system. The dog whined anxiously and scratched at the truck door, trying to get out.

"Knock it off, Silk. No one is home," she told him. She thought about working her way up the unplowed driveway, just to make sure the Malones were all right, but just as she opened the door of the truck, Scott paged her on the police radio.

"Carly, I need you back here with the truck. Smitty needs help getting some groceries delivered, and I told him we'd pitch in."

She closed the truck door, "No problem, Scott. I'll head back now."

She cast a last glance at the Malone house before she started the truck up again. As she backed up, she saw crows on the property again, perched in the old tree in front of the house and on the road facing peak of the roof.

"Must be some food attracting those birds," she thought aloud.

"Wonder if there is a dead animal near the house."

She began to tremble, and the cold-all-over feeling suddenly engulfed her. She jacked the truck heater up as high as it would go before turning around to head back. The snow had started falling heavily again, coating the plowed roads with an icy coat. Silk whined all the way back.

SEVENTEEN

It was four o'clock by the time Carly got home, and Scott was picking her up at five thirty. She took a shower and dressed quickly, deciding to wear the sweater her mother had given her for her birthday. It was a deep shade of forest green cashmere, which was a perfect complement to her auburn hair and green eyes. She finished the outfit with a new camel-colored wool skirt and some new brown dress boots. Instead of her usual ponytail, she let her hair fall in loose curls around her shoulders.

"Not bad," she told herself as she appraised her image in the mirror. "Not bad at all."

Scott arrived exactly on time, and she could tell by the way he looked at her that he liked what he saw. He turned beet red when he realized that she had picked up on his admiring glances.

Scott was dressed in a brown tweed blazer with leather elbow patches and a leather collar. He had an ivory-colored turtleneck sweater under it and dark brown pants. The look was a far cry from his khaki police uniform. "We'll show everyone we can dress like normal people. Maybe they won't recognize us," he said as he helped her with her coat.

Carly bent down and gave Silk a quick hug and closed the door. Scott took her hand to help her down the icy steps. She liked the feel of her hand in his and gave just the slightest squeeze back to let him know.

The Grange Hall was brightly lit, and wonderful aromas greeted them when they opened the big double door. Baked hams, beans simmering in rich molasses sauces, macaroni and cheese casseroles, and homemade apple pies lined the long banquet tables, exactly what Carly expected—comfort food. There was a cash bar near the stage, and people milled around it, chatting as they waited for their drinks. They looked around the hall before finding two seats at one of the round tables near the stage where they joined Smitty and his wife, Ruth, and Tommy Riley and his wife, Angela. Carly was happy to see them in a social gathering instead of talking to them across a counter or at a cash register.

"Carly, what can I get you to drink?" Scott asked.

"Just a glass of red wine, Scott. That will be fine," she said.

She scanned the room to see if the Malones had come but didn't spot them anywhere. Scott returned with their drinks, and along with the others at the table, they raised a toast to the evening. A three-piece band showed up around eight thirty and played a medley of good dance tunes. Several couples headed for the dance floor as soon as the music started, and most of the crowd joined in after a few sets.

"Carly, would you like to dance?" Scott asked her.

"I'd love to, Scott," she said, taking his hand as they headed for the dance floor. The band was playing a slow romantic number from the fifties, and Scott pulled Carly into him, his arm hugging her waist, his hand enveloping hers against his shoulder. She hadn't danced with anyone except Rob in a very long time and felt uneasy in the arms of someone else. Scott felt her tension and cajoled her into getting comfortable. "Relax, Carly. I promise I won't step on your toes," he said as he guided her into a slow dance across the floor.

"Sorry, Scott. I haven't done this in a while." She closed her eyes and leaned her head on his shoulder as they danced to the soft music, feeling warm and safe for the first time in months. Easing her body into Scott's, she enjoyed the feeling of closeness as they moved in perfect unison. Dancing with him felt natural, and she finally relaxed, letting herself move to his lead.

The band quit at eleven thirty, and after saying good-bye to everyone, Scott and Carly headed for his car. He walked her to entrance of her condo, and she extended her hand, thanking him.

"I had a really nice time tonight, Scott. I'm glad I went. Thank you for a lovely evening." He pulled her to him and surprised her with a gentle kiss. She responded back to him, liking the feeling of his mouth on hers, his arms around her waist. All the while she was thinking, *This is not a good idea! This is not a good idea!*

Eighteen

Carly spent most of Sunday catching up on neglected chores. Scott called her in the afternoon to thank her again for a lovely evening, hinting that he would like to take her out again. She had enjoyed being with him but her emotional bond to Rob had not weakened and she was reluctant to get more deeply involved with another man, especially one with whom she worked every day.

Kate Malone had been on her mind all that day, and she tried several times, unsuccessfully, to reach her on her cell phone.

Maybe they've gone away for the weekend, she thought. *Maybe her cell phone is turned off. I should have stopped to check on them when I was there.*

She fixed a quick supper of bacon and eggs, made a pot of tea, and settled into the old armchair, wrapping herself in a woolen throw. Silk curled up on the sofa, nesting into the plush cushions. Scott called her again, checking to see if she was all right. He was just leaving the department office and closing up for the night. Carly sensed that he might have liked an invitation to spend the night but she brushed him off quickly, telling him she would see him in the morning.

She hung up and immediately tried Kate one more time. Still no answer. She had been feeling guilty about not calling her parents for a couple of weeks and decided to make that call while it was on her mind but secretly hoped that they weren't home. The phone rang a couple of times before Hannah picked up and Carly gritted her teeth before she spoke.

"Hi, Mama. It's Carly. Just thought I would call and say hello."

"Carly, dear, how nice to hear your voice. I was just talking about you this afternoon to Phyllis Burns. She's the country club owner's wife, you know. She was very interested in what you were doing, so of course I had to tell her how successful you are in your new position and all. Oh, and Pastor Middleton's daughter had her baby finally. A little girl. And your father and I are invited to the christening. Won't that be lovely? Your father is getting so fat, dear. I've had to put him on a diet. Cut out all sugar and those horrible donuts he likes. I've been going to the women's club gym twice a week just to keep my weight the same. It's so easy to put on weight when you get older. You should watch it too, dear. You know you always had a tendency to get a little pudgy. Oh, and I've joined another bridge club, and honestly these women are too serious about the game. My goodness, if you make the slightest mistake, they are just all over you about it. I am thinking I may not stay in this group for much longer." Hannah took a quick breath. "And how are *you*, dear?"

Carly had all she could do to keep screaming with exasperation. "I thought you'd never ask! I'm good, Mama. The weather hasn't been great, but I still like it here a lot, and—"

True to form, Hannah interrupted. "The weather has been lovely here, dear. We've had a beautiful fall and haven't had to turn the heat on at all yet. Can you believe that? And here it is almost Thanksgiving. We are going to stay home again this year, dear. I suppose you have to work and won't be able to come, but do let me know if your plans change. Oh, your father just came in, dear. I have to go. Nice to talk to you. Do call more often, dear, won't you? Good-bye now."

Hannah hung up before Carly could get another word in. She stood holding the phone in her hand.

"Nice to talk to you too, Mama," she said as she put the phone back in its cradle.

She fell asleep in the chair around eight o'clock with the TV still on. The nightmare started again just as the weather forecast was issuing another storm warning.

She was more than halfway up the driveway now, but the house seemed to be moving further away with each labored step she took. The wind howled through the barren tree branches, sending streamers of snow whirling around her. She lurched forward, desperate to reach the house. She could hear the old barn groaning and creaking from the weight of the snow on its roof and the pummeling of the wind on its sides. She called for Kate again and again, her voice drowned by the banshee cries of the wind. She was out of breath, and her chest hurt from breathing the frigid air. The snow was so heavy that she could no longer see the lights of the house. She stopped and turned around, wanting to head back, but she was trapped by the great drifts that had piled around her. She couldn't see beyond the reach of her arm, and she was deafened by the screaming wind. Standing fast in the deep drift, she wept great icy tears while two crows circled overhead, riding the wind draughts. Their beady yellow eyes never shifted their gaze from her face.

NINETEEN

M onday morning announced itself with the shrill call of the alarm clock at exactly 5:30 a.m., startling Carly from a deep sleep. She sat wide-eyed for a minute before she realized that she had slept in the old armchair all night. She knew that she dreamt the same dream that frightened her a few nights before. The memory of it was still sharp, and she sat for a moment, trying to put the pieces of it together to make some sense of it. It reminded her of the jigsaw puzzles she had loved to do when she was a child. But she couldn't seem to find any pieces that fit together in these dreams. She knew deep down that they were connected, but she couldn't figure the pattern out.

Scott was already at the building when Carly arrived. She walked in to the smell of fresh coffee, warm donuts, and the comforting heat of a crackling woodstove.

He shouted from the back office when he heard her come in. "Mornin', Carly. Looks like another beautiful November day!"

"Yup, I am beginning to love this weather. Was I just dreaming that there were four seasons up here?" She shouted back sarcastically.

Scott came out to the front office and poured two cups of coffee. They sat eating sugar-frosted donuts while planning the day's work. No mention was made about Saturday night even though they were each eager to talk about it.

They finished the day's schedule around eight o'clock, deciding to meet up for lunch if time permitted. Carly still couldn't get Kate off her mind, so she picked up the phone and dialed Malone's home number. To Carly's surprise, Kate answered after a couple of rings. Carly's sigh of relief filled the small office.

"Kate, it's Carly. I've been trying to reach you since I left your place on Saturday. Are you guys okay? I drove by yesterday, and it didn't look like Sean had plowed you out. Do you need some help out there?"

"No, we're fine, Carly, really," Kate said.

"Sean's had a cold, and I didn't want him to go out in that awful weather and get chilled."

Carly could hear some muffled noise in the background, and it sounded as if Maura was crying.

"What's going on with Maura, Katie? Sounds like she got hurt."

"No, no, Carly. Just playing. That's all. We all have a touch of cabin fever from being cooped in all weekend. Listen, I really have to go now. But before I forget, we want you to come for Thanksgiving dinner with us. Can you make it?"

Carly hesitated before answering, not sure if that was the way she wanted to spend the holiday. But she didn't want to disappoint Kate, so she accepted the invitation.

"I'd love to, Kate," Carly replied. "What can I bring?"

"Not a thing. Just yourself, Carly, and Silk. Gotta go now."

Kate hurried to end the conversation and hung up before Carly had a chance to say good-bye. Kate had made sure to clear the invitation with Sean before inviting Carly and was surprised that he agreed to it. She had caught him on one of his very rare "good moments" and hoped that he wouldn't change his mind as the holiday got closer.

Scott overheard the conversation and was curious to find out how things were going at Lakeview Farm.

"Couldn't help eavesdropping, Carly. Is everything okay with the Malones?" he asked.

"Kate is sure trying hard to make me think so! I just got an invitation to spend Thanksgiving Day with them."

Scott's expression changed, and he was visibly disappointed in Carly's answer.

"She beat me to it! I was going to ask you to spend Thanksgiving Day with *me*," he said.

Carly wished she hadn't accepted Kate's invitation so quickly, especially since she could have spent the day with Scott.

"What if I ask her if you can come along with me? Would you go?"

"Well, I'd like to be with you, but I think it's probably better for you to go alone. We can catch up and maybe spend the evening together. How's that?" he asked.

"I think I would like that a lot," Carly replied.

"Probably better not to overwhelm Sean with too much company anyway. He's such an antisocial bastard as it is. I honestly don't want to go, but I hate to disappoint Kate. Are you sure you don't mind, Scott?"

"Hey, I'd rather spend the evening with you anyway. No worries. I have plenty I can do during the day. I might even bake a pie," he said.

TWENTY

The weather mellowed somewhat just before Thanksgiving Day. Snow still covered the ground in drifts, but a few days of sun here and there had melted some areas to near-bare ground. The townspeople were getting ready for Thanksgiving and the holiday season, and the whole mood of Saint Basile changed from dismal to cheerful almost overnight.

Carly wasn't looking forward to spending Thanksgiving with the Malones, but she had made the commitment and would stick with it. On her next day off, she drove into Burlington to shop for some house gifts to bring to them for the holiday. Burlington was overflowing with people shopping for the holidays and UVM students hanging out at the coffee shops and little boutique restaurants. Carly wandered in and out of a few of the shops before she found some large pillar candles and two good bottles of wine for Kate and some Magic Hat beer for Sean. She spotted a little side street gift shop where she found a beautiful handmade Raggedy Ann doll for Maura. The doll was meticulously made with black button eyes and a broad embroidered smiling mouth. Bright red yarn covered the cloth head, and a crisp white apron fit over the blue calico dress. Carly turned the doll over, admiring the quality of the workmanship and the attention to detail. Maura will love this, she thought.

On the way back to the parking lot, she stopped in a small food market and picked up a cooked turkey breast and some stuffing and vegetables. There was a wine display at the rear of the store, and she grabbed a bottle of California Chardonnay to go with the turkey.

It was getting dark, and it starting to snow again, so Carly headed right back to her car and her waiting dog, anxious to get home before the driving got bad. By the time she reached Saint Basile, two inches of powdery snow had covered the roads, and she could see the plows just beginning to line up for the first pass along the highway.

The day before Thanksgiving, Carly called Kate to confirm dinnertime. It took Kate a while to pick up the phone, and Carly thought she sounded distracted when she answered.

"Kate, it's Carly. Just checking on dinnertime for tomorrow."

"Oh, sure Carly. I was going to call you tonight. How about you come around three, and we can have a drink before dinner?'

"Sounds good to me. Can I bring anything?"

"Oh, no. Please don't. I have everything here. Just bring yourself. We are anxious to see you."

"Okay, but call me if you think of anything. I'll see you tomorrow."

Carly didn't like the way Kate sounded, but she dismissed it as Kate just being tired.

She called Scott to confirm their plans for the following evening, hoping that she could break away from the Malones by seven o'clock. He was still at the department office, and it took him a while to answer the phone.

"Scott, it's just me. Are you busy right now?"

"Hi, Carly. I was just thinking about you! Not busy, no. I was out back in the cellblock just checking on one of the cell doors. It seems to come unlatched if there is the slightest power surge. Must be a circuit problem or something. I'm calling the maintenance guys in to check it. What's up?"

"I just wanted to confirm for tomorrow night," she said. "I should be home by seven thirty, and I thought maybe we could have a light supper. I have some nice wine that I bought in

Burlington today, and I actually picked up a small turkey breast that I will cook tonight. We can pretend its leftovers!"

"That should work just fine for me," he said. "I'm looking forward to a quiet evening!"

After they said good-bye, Carly wondered if the evening was going to linger beyond the light supper. Part of her hoped that it would, and part of her was afraid that it might. She was pretty sure that Scott was attracted to her, and she had begun to feel something for him that went way beyond a working relationship. Thanksgiving evening would be memorable for more reasons than just spending the first holiday in her new place. Carly was sure of it.

TWENTY-ONE

Thanksgiving Day started out with bright sunshine and moderate temperatures for late November. A few wispy clouds dotted the sky, and although there was a forecast for a late-afternoon snowfall, nothing ominous was on the horizon that morning. Carly got up early and headed to the office to check for messages. Scott had taken the day off, and she was on call. When she got there, she found that Scott had already responded to the three messages that were on the machine, so she checked all the doors and windows, set the temperature a little lower, and had the phone system forward any additional calls directly to her cell phone. She locked up and headed home to get ready to go to the Malone's.

The minute she opened her back door, she saw her answering machine winking at her from the kitchen counter. There was a message from her mother, which made her grimace when she heard the familiar high-pitched voice.

"Carly? Are you there, dear? Pick up if you are there. Oh, I suppose you are out, or you just don't want to talk to me. Just want to wish you happy Thanksgiving, dear. Daddy does too. We are fine. Hope you are too, dear. Well, that's all I wanted to say. Call us if you have a minute."

Carly picked up the phone and started to dial her parents' phone number, but she hung up on the third digit. She felt badly about the strained relationship with her parents, but at the same time, she was happy to have avoided spending a holiday feeling awkward and uncomfortable for the whole day. Aside from a few brief phone calls, contact between Carly and her parents had been limited since she left Massachusetts. Her father continued to refuse to speak with her, and she, being just as stubborn, didn't make any overtures to him that would mend the breach.

She tried to reach Rachel, but there was no answer, so she left a voice message for her, then headed for her bedroom to wrap the gifts she had picked up for the Malones. Pulling Raggedy Ann from the bag, she held the doll out in front of her for a moment then propped her up in the rocking chair near the window while she wrapped up the wine and beer gifts. The doll stared at her with her shiny black button eyes and enigmatic smile. The button eyes seemed to follow her, and for a brief second, Carly thought that the embroidered mouth widened its red grin. *Impossible*, she thought.

She picked the doll up again, shook the wrinkles from the dress, and looked it over for any imperfections. Satisfied that it was in perfect condition, she spread some tissue paper out to wrap the doll.

"I hope Maura likes you, Raggedy. I really do," she said to it as she placed it on the bed.

Silk seemed overly curious about the doll, sniffing and nudging at its cloth body. Carly pushed him away from it.

"C'mon, Silk. Get away from her. What's the matter with you?" The dog circled around Carly, his eyes fixed on the doll, his hackles raised. Carly pushed him away again and laid the doll on the tissue paper spread out on the bed, wrapping it carefully before putting it back in the canvas bag. Silk nuzzled at the bag a few times before moving away from it. Carly wondered what had gotten into him. He tried to get the bag off the bed and kept tugging at the handles to move it toward the edge of the comforter.

"No, Silk. Stop it! What's wrong with you, you silly dog? Come away from that doll right now. That's not a toy for you if that's what you're thinking."

Silk looked at her as he backed away, his eyes never leaving the canvas tote bag.

TWENTY-TWO

Carly left her place around two o'clock on Thanksgiving Day and didn't pass a single car all the way to the Malone farm. An armada of huge gray clouds pushed across the already darkened sky, promising to deliver yet another barrage of snow and ice before the day was done. There were no streetlamps along the road, and the only light Carly had was from her car headlamps. Lakeview Farm sat on a small hill, and as she got closer to the property, she could see the house lights casting yellow beams across the snow-covered ground in front of the house. Smoke was billowing in white puffs from the fireplace chimney, and the gas lanterns along the driveway flickered a welcome as she drove in. She noticed the ever-present crows again perched along the fence. Silk spotted them as well and sent out a warning bark, which scattered them to flight, their black wings flapping wildly in the cold air.

Carly parked beside Sean's pickup and headed for the back door, gifts stuffed into two large canvas bags. The kitchen window was cracked open a bit, and Carly could smell the roasting meat in the oven and freshly baked pies cooling on the windowsill. Kate saw her at the back door and opened it quickly, greeting her with a beaming smile.

"Carly, I am *so* happy that you could come today. Come in, come in. Give me your jacket."

Carly hugged Kate and handed her the two gift bags and her jacket. Maura spotted Carly and came running into the kitchen, red curls bouncing around her freckled face. "Carly! Carly!" she squealed. "Come see my dollhouse. Come play with me!"

She had Carly by the sleeve of her sweater and dragged her into the family room where Sean was watching a Thanksgiving football game.

"Hi, Sean," Carly called out, trying to sound cheerful. "How are you?"

He mumbled something back, never once looking at her. She followed Maura across the room to look at the dollhouse sitting on the floor near the stairs. Silk followed and found a spot near Maura's dollhouse, settling down after making a few obligatory nesting circles.

"Maura," Carly said, "If you go out to the kitchen and bring back the two green bags, I think you may find something in there that you'll like. Tell Mama to come back with you, too."

Maura scrambled out of the room, rushing to the kitchen. Kate came back in with her and sat on the sofa beside Sean while Carly opened the bags. The dog was up now, running from one side to another, tail wagging madly from side to side. Carly handed the wine, beer, and candles to Kate.

"Just a little something for the host and hostess."

Carly pulled Raggedy Ann out of the bag, still wrapped in the white tissue, and handed her to Maura, who shouted with delight and hugged the doll tightly as she danced across the room with it. Silk tried to get at the doll again as he had done back at Carly's place.

"Silk, get away from there!" Carly yelled. "I don't know what's got into him lately. He is acting really strange around this doll," she said to Kate.

Kate laughed. "Maybe he thinks it's a new chew toy, Carly. It's a beautiful doll! You shouldn't have done all this. You spent way too much money on us."

"My pleasure, Kate," Carly replied. "Be quiet and enjoy!"

Kate gave Sean a subtle nudge, trying to get him to show some appreciation for the gifts. His eyes were glued to the TV football game, but he turned away for a second, said something unintelligible, and turned back to watching the TV. *Sullen cur*, Carly thought to herself. She was starting to seriously dislike Sean Malone and was trying hard not to show it.

Kate was visibly disturbed by Sean's behavior, and Carly sensed that she was on the verge of saying something to him about it. She grabbed Kate by the elbow and moved her toward the kitchen.

"C'mon, Katie girl, let's get that dinner fixed. The natives will be getting hungry."

Kate flashed Carly a grateful smile, and the two headed toward the kitchen doorway.

"Kate, I've been meaning to ask you something," Carly said. "Whenever I come here, I notice a bunch of crows hanging around, either on the fence or sometimes up on the roof peak. Are you feeding them or something?"

"No. I am actually chasing them away all the time. They sit on that fence and bicker all day. The sounds they make really give me the creeps. I've never liked those birds anyway, but I can't seem to get rid of them. There must be food or something lying about that keeps them coming back every day."

"That's what I was thinking. They usually hang around if there is something dead they can pick on. Maybe there's a dead animal near the house someplace," Carly suggested.

"I don't know. I've looked everywhere. And they seem to just sit on the damn fence all day, watching. Creepy-looking things!"

While they were talking, Kate bent over to pick up a dishtowel from the floor. Carly was still talking to her when she noticed several large bruises on the backs of Kate's legs, just below her skirt hemline.

She stopped and caught Kate by the elbow, turning her around.

"Kate, what happened to your legs?" she asked. "They're all bruised up in the back."

Kate looked away from Carly before she answered. "I'm so clumsy lately. I fell in the barn the other day. That's all. My fault for not looking where I was going. Tripped over the stupid manure rakes and landed on one of the loft steps." She changed the subject quickly, and Carly knew that the conversation was closed, but she had the same feeling that came over her the last time she noticed bruises on Kate. She was positive now that Kate was lying to her about the bruises, but she didn't feel that she could pursue the issue any further just then.

Carly found the rabbit corkscrew on the counter and opened up one of the wine bottles, pouring a glass for Kate and herself. Kate had prepared a beautiful dinner, and Carly could tell that a lot of time had gone into that preparation. The turkey was roasted to a golden brown, and there were bowls of vegetables lined up on the counter along with a large casserole dish filled with stuffing. They were at the sink, raising their glasses together in a toast when Sean yelled from the family room.

"Kate! When is that stupid dinner going to be ready? I'm starving, and so is Maura. You've had all day to get it ready."

Kate froze in place at the sink. Without turning around, she stiffened her back, collecting herself.

"It's done, Sean. We are just getting it ready to bring to the dining table," she called back.

Maura appeared in the doorway, Raggedy Ann under one arm.

"Want me to help, Mummy?" she asked.

"No, honey. Carly is helping, and we are almost ready to put things on the table. Why don't you go and wash up?"

The little girl stood still in the doorway, eyes brimming with tears, hugging the doll tightly to her little chest.

"What's wrong, baby?" Carly asked.

"I don't want to go back in there, Carly, because Daddy's mad again. Will you come with me, please?"

"Sure, I will, honey."

Carly shot Kate a questioning look before taking Maura by the hand and going into the family room, careful to avoid passing in front of Sean as they headed for the staircase. She was thinking that this dinner invitation was turning out to be a bad idea and wished that she had refused it. Sean was obviously in a vile mood, Kate was tense, and Maura was afraid to go back into the room where her father was sitting. Almost at the stairs, Maura tripped on a corner of the rug and knocked over a small wooden table behind Sean's chair. He jumped up from his seat, shaking his fist at the little girl.

"Maura, will you knock it off! I'm trying to watch the game, and if you don't stop making noise, I'm going to smack you," Sean yelled.

Maura stopped where she was, looking with confusion from Sean to Carly, and then proceeded on tiptoe to the upstairs bathroom.

"Sean," Carly said, "she just tripped. Lighten up!"

Sean was still standing, and he turned and faced Carly with an icy stare. "It's none of your business, Carly, so just butt out. I'm sick of you sticking your nose in stuff around here. She's my kid, and I'll talk to her the way I want to."

He was red-faced with rage, and obviously, he had had too much to drink.

Carly was stunned to silence. Without responding back to Sean, she headed back to the kitchen just as Kate was taking the turkey to the dining room. Carly grabbed the wine bottle and poured two more glasses without saying a word about what just happened in the family room.

TWENTY-THREE

Dinner went from bad to worse, and Carly bided her time until she could give a good excuse to make an early exit. Sean barely said a word, other than to complain that the turkey was overcooked. Maura was close to tears during the whole meal and asked to be excused from the table before dessert was served. Kate was a nervous wreck and chattered nonstop about nothing. When Sean got up to go back to the football games on TV, Carly got ready to leave. She helped Kate clear the table, and when they had finished the dishes, she decided it would be a good time to break away.

"Kate, that was a wonderful meal, but I really can't stay any longer. The weather report doesn't look good, and it's already starting to snow. I hate driving at night in the stuff, so would you mind if I get ready to leave now?"

She could see the disappointment wash over Kate's face.

"Oh, of course not, Carly. I understand. I hate to drive in it myself." Kate was visibly disappointed, but she made no effort to coax Carly into staying longer.

When they finished in the kitchen, Carly headed into the family room to say good-bye to Sean and Maura. Sean was sitting alone, and Maura had gone upstairs, dragging Raggedy Ann with her. Carly said good-bye to Sean, who never looked up from the TV, and went back to the kitchen to get her coat. Silk knew she was getting ready to go, and he jumped around excitedly at the kitchen door. Kate watched him, thinking that he sensed the tension in the house as well and was anxious to get out of there.

"Kate, thanks again for dinner. I really appreciated the invitation. I'll call you soon. Maybe we can meet in town for lunch one of these days."

"That would be nice, Carly. Let's do that," Kate managed a weak little smile and a good-bye hug.

Carly knew that the lunch would never take place.

Sean stayed slouched in his recliner chair, staring blankly at the football game on the TV. Kate finished putting the dishes away then headed into the family room. She sat on the sofa beside Sean's chair and put her hand on his arm.

"Sean, what's wrong? I had so hoped that we could have a nice dinner today. You were really rude to Carly, and I was embarrassed. What's the matter? I don't know what to do anymore. Nothing I do ever pleases you, and you are at poor Maura all the time. Please tell me what's wrong."

Sean looked at her and for a moment she thought he was going to start a fight again, but his eyes filled with tears and he got up from his chair and sat beside her on the sofa.

"Katie, I don't know what's wrong with me. I'm sorry about today, I really am. I don't know what comes over me sometimes. I have nothing against Carly or any of your other friends. I just don't like Carly hanging around here so much, seeing that she's a cop and all. Makes me nervous, I guess." Kate reluctantly accepted his apology but deep down she had the feeling that he really didn't mean it. There was something he wasn't telling her, something about his feelings towards Carly that went way beyond her being a police officer.

The snow was falling heavily when Carly left to head home. The Malone's driveway was already slick, and the road was in worse condition. She put the car into four-wheel drive and eased it onto the main road, cautiously heading back toward town. Squalls were swirling across the vacant meadows on either side of the road, and the conditions were near whiteout. Carly put her fog lights on as she struggled to see the way in front of her. It took her nearly an hour to get back to town, a ride that was usually only fifteen minutes. The plows had not been out yet, and snow was piling up everywhere, driven by a biting wind. For a moment, an image from the night of the accident flashed through her mind. The weather conditions were nearly the same, and she started shivering all over as she tried to block the horrible sounds of metal scraping against metal that were filling her head.

The car skidded as she entered the condo parking lot, and she had to adjust quickly to avoid hitting any other cars already parked there. The space markers were barely visible, but she was able to ease into her assigned space as closely as she could.

"I don't know if I can take much more of this weather, Silk," she complained to the dog. "It's dragging me down. I used to love snow, but I am starting to really hate it!"

Scott pulled in just behind her, and she let out a sigh of relief, happy to see him. He grabbed her arm, helping her maneuver the slick walkway as they inched their way to the condo.

"I'm so glad you're here," she told him. "I just had the most horrible day you can imagine. That Malone family is a ticking time bomb, Scott. Something's going to happen out there. I feel it every time I'm with them."

Scott could see that she was upset.

"You can tell me all about it when we get inside, okay?" he said. "Too damn cold to stay out here and talk!"

Carly could see the message light on her telephone winking at her from the kitchen.

"Scott, just let me check my messages. Looks like there are a few on the answering machine."

There was a message from Rachel as well as one from her mother. She decided that she had better return Hannah's call before the night ran out.

"Hi, Mama, it's Carly," she said when Hannah answered the phone. "Happy Thanksgiving. Just returning your call. Hope you had a nice dinner."

"Well, hello, dear! Your father and I were just beginning to think we wouldn't hear from you today at all. I thought we would hear from you much earlier than this. I thought maybe you had forgotten all about your poor old parents. We had dinner alone here, but of course, I cooked the usual huge meal. I think we may go out next year if you decide not to spend the holidays with us, and I do hope you won't decide that. And by the way, what about Christmas? Are you coming home for Christmas? It was a bit lonesome today. It is a good thing that I am so busy with the guild, and Daddy is working all the time at the firm these days. And I suppose you are working yourself to the bone in that terrible weather up there. I wish you would call more often, dear. We hardly hear from you anymore. And before I forget, Mrs. Carter passed away last week. You remember her, dear, don't you? Her husband owns that lovely little restaurant downtown. Such a shame, really."

And so it went for fifteen minutes. The calls were always the same, always one-sided and always unimportant. Carly looked over at Scott, rolling her eyes in exasperation at the nonstop chatter from her mother.

"Mama, take a breath! I won't be home for Christmas unless Daddy decides he wants to speak to me. And since I am pretty sure he doesn't want to speak to me, then I guess I won't be home anytime soon!"

Silence at the other end.

Carly broke the awkwardness of the moment, feeling bad that she had taken her frustration out on her mother.

"So aren't you going to ask how I am, Mama?"

"Well, of course I am, dear, you didn't give me a chance." Hannah sighed. "How are you?"

"I'm good, actually, and very happy up here," Carly replied. "The weather has been rotten, but we are all dealing with it. You and Daddy are certainly welcome to come here for Christmas as long as he is over his pout by then."

Hannah sputtered a bit.

"I'll ask your father, but I don't think he will want to drive all the way up there especially if you have all that awful snow around. I'll ask and let you know, dear."

Carly knew the answer already, secretly hoping that they would not make the trip.

"Okay, Mama. Let me know. I have another call coming in, so let's talk soon."

Carly hung up, heaving a long sigh.

Scott couldn't help listening to the one-sided conversation, wondering exactly what had happened in Carly's life before she arrived in Saint Basile. He could tell from the tone of the conversation that her relationship with her parents was strained, but he suspected that there were other monsters hiding in Carly's closet as well. He poured a glass of wine for each of them and motioned for Carly to join him on the couch. He had overheard the conversation with her mother, and she decided that it was time to fill him in about her family and also about her reasons for being in Saint Basile in the first place. Scott gave her the opening she needed.

"That didn't sound like a happy holiday call, Carly. Want to tell me what's going on?" he asked.

She settled in beside him, and he placed his arm around her shoulder.

"This may take more than a glass of wine, Scott. Are you sure you want all the gory details?"

"Yeah, I do, Carly. I don't know anything about you at all, and I promise, whatever you tell me won't run me off, okay?"

She gave him a quick kiss on the cheek, took a sip of wine, and began to tell him who Charlotte Richardson really was.

"Well, you've probably already guessed that there is a problem between me and my parents. That started years ago, but it came to a head when I took this job. I love my mother, don't get me wrong, but she drives me nuts. She means well, but she never shuts up, and she is more concerned with what her friends think than with anything else. She's oblivious to anything that doesn't concern her directly, which is why I hate to get on the phone with her. It's never a conversation. It's just her giving me a report about her. And my father? Well, he's the total opposite. Quiet, very stern and very uncompromising. He literally planned out my entire career before I knew what was happening. He's a senior partner in a Boston law firm and fully expected me to work my way up to a partnership with him. I never got a chance to do anything I wanted to do when I was growing up. In fact, up until the time I came here, he was still trying to control my life. I had a great job at his law firm, with good pay, but it wasn't what I wanted to do. It was what he wanted me to do. He was so difficult to deal with all the time, and our relationship really soured toward the end. And added to all this drama, I'm an only child, and for every unfulfilled hope and dream they ever had, they looked to me to make them all come true. No pressure or anything!"

"So all that doesn't sound like enough to drive you away. What was it that forced you to decide to leave?" Scott asked. "Jack and I couldn't figure out what would have brought you all the way up here, especially when you had such a good job in Boston."

The subject of her engagement to Rob had never come up, and she knew she had to tell him about it. She told him everything, including the details of the accident and what it did to her emotionally. Scott listened intently as the story unfolded. When she finished, Carly turned to look at him, watching for his reaction. He remained quiet and just held her tightly, not knowing what to say.

"I haven't talked about this in a long time, Scott. But now you know about the baggage that came along to Saint Basile with me. And it doesn't go away. I've been plagued by nightmares ever since the accident. They are more frequent now, and I think it is because the weather has been so bad. They're always about snow, and I wake up shaking as if something bad is going to happen. The strange thing is that now they seem to be connected to Lakeview Farm for some reason. I keep dreaming that I am trying to get into the house to get Kate, but the snow is so deep that I can't move. And when I am able to move, the house seems to get further away, so I can't ever reach it. And there are these horrible birds all the time. Huge black crows, staring at me with ugly yellow eyes. Like the ones that are sitting on the fence out there all the time."

She suddenly felt tired and leaned back against Scott's shoulder. He turned and took her face gently in both his hands. "I'm still here, Carly. You didn't scare me away, and I'm glad you told me all this. I've known for a while that there was something lying just beneath the surface with you."

He kissed her gently and then again with more intensity. She pushed him back at first, then her emotions took over, and she returned his kiss with an urgency she hadn't felt in months.

"Scott, we shouldn't be doing this," she whispered to him. "We work together. This isn't a good thing."

He silenced her with another kiss, running his hands along her body until he could feel her relax under his caress. Carly was caught up in the passion of the moment and lay back on the sofa, pulling Scott down to her in a tight embrace. Their lovemaking was slow and tender, and for a short time, Carly's problems were washed away. When it was over, they lay still in each other's arms, neither one wanting to move. It was Carly who finally interrupted the mood. She grabbed the afghan from the back of the sofa and wrapped it around her while she collected her clothes from the floor. She suddenly felt awkward and tried to act as if nothing had happened.

"I almost forgot, Scott. I have a small dinner still keeping warm in the oven! I don't know about you, but I'm hungry."

Scott groaned a little, not wanting to get up, but since Carly had already gone into her bedroom to get her robe, he got dressed and headed for the kitchen to see if he could help.

Carly had set the table earlier that day, so all she had to do was put the turkey and vegetables out to be served. Scott opened the wine she had purchased, and when they sat down, he raised his glass in a toast. "Here's to us, Carly, and to a thousand nights like this in our futures." Carly blushed and clinked her glass with his, echoing his wish back.

It was after ten o'clock by the time they finished dinner. Although neither one brought the subject up, it was a given that Scott would be spending the night. By eleven o'clock, they were snuggled into her bed under the down comforter, watching the snowflakes tumbling past the bedroom window. Silk was curled up on the floor beside the bed while Carly drifted off to sleep, wrapped in Scott's arms. Scott lay looking at her, tracing the outline of her face with his fingers. He was captivated by this woman, and he admitted to himself that he was falling in love with her. He hadn't planned it. It just happened. He also knew that she wasn't ready for commitment to anyone just yet, but he was willing to wait. His mind was running at full speed, and he lay awake for a long time, watching the snow tumbling like popped corn from the black sky.

TWENTY-FOUR

Carly had only been asleep for an hour when the dream intruded on her again and unraveled her rest.

She was pounding on a door and shouting for Kate to open it. It was snowing hard. The two black crows glared down at her from their perch on the door lintel, squawking each time she put her fist to the door. She could see Kate in the kitchen by the sink, watching the snow gather against the frosted windowpanes.

Carly pounded until her hands were bleeding through her mittens, blood freezing as it came through the white wool, staining it bright crimson. She saw Sean coming into the kitchen, his "Life Is Crap" T-shirt stained all over with dark splotches. "Let me in, Sean!" she screamed. "Let me in right now!" He never looked at the door. He just walked toward Kate with something in his hand. Carly couldn't see his face clearly, nor could she see what he was holding. She pounded and kicked and screamed at the locked door. She tried to break the glass panes with her bloodied hands, but the glass wouldn't crack. Sean moved in slow motion toward Kate, who was still transfixed by the storm outside. Kate turned to face Carly. Her face was smeared with blood, and her shiny black button eyes stared in vacant surprise at Carly's frightened face in the door window. Kate could see that what Sean had in his hand was the Raggedy Ann doll. He propped it up in the wooden kitchen chair so that it faced the door, its eyeless face smiling wickedly at Carly.

She woke up screaming and drenched in perspiration, frightened by the sound of her own voice. Her scream startled Scott, and he jumped up, wondering what had happened. The dog was at the foot of the bed, trembling, a low growl coming from deep in his throat. The green LED display on the alarm clock registered 4:30 a.m. Friday morning. Carly was motionless, still wrapped in the white goose down comforter. She could see that the snow was still coming down heavily, whipped about by gusts of wind. She was perspiring and freezing at the same time, her shivers rattling the bed. Scott felt helpless, not knowing what had happened or how to fix it.

"Carly, for God's sake, what's wrong? What frightened you?"

She sat up, still trembling.

"That nightmare. I had that nightmare again. I don't know what's wrong, Scott. I can't seem to stop it."

He gathered her in his arms, holding her tightly to stop her shivering.

"It's okay, it's okay. Just a bad dream," he said, talking to her as if she were a child.

They lay back for a few minutes.

Carly turned to check the clock, realizing that they had to get ready for work.

"I'm sorry you had to be wakened that way, Scott. Not very romantic, was it? I'm so embarrassed, and I feel downright stupid. Come on, we have to get moving, or we'll be late for work. Look at the time."

She wanted to get his attention off her and on to the morning ahead, so she got up quickly and threw on her robe and slippers before he had a chance to say anything else. She managed to get herself into the kitchen, where she brewed a fresh pot of coffee and fed Silk. Scott showered and joined her at the table.

"Feeling better?" he asked.

"I think so. God, I wish they would stop. I am so tired from not getting enough sleep."

She really did start to feel better after the second cup of coffee and decided she would bring up the subject that they were both trying to avoid. "Scott, about last night…"

He interrupted her before she could say anything else.

"Carly, whatever it is that may be bothering you about last night, including being embarrassed by your dream, I want you to put it aside. Something special happened between us, and I don't want to spoil that. I don't think you do either," he said.

"I don't want to spoil it, Scott. I just worry because we work together, and you know how people talk. Something tells me that we shouldn't be crossing this line. Aren't you concerned at all?"

"As a matter of fact, no," he said. "I'm not a bit concerned, and I don't care what other people think. I only care about what *you* think, Carly," he replied.

"I think I felt real again last night for the first time in ages. And I feel…well, I feel *right* with you. I just don't know where this might take us or if I'm ready to go."

They finished breakfast and headed for work in their separate vehicles. Both had promised to help with some of the town holiday projects that would already be underway. They agreed to meet up at the end of the day near the Christmas tree in the town commons.

Saint Basile always decorated for Christmas on the day after Thanksgiving, regardless of what the weather conditions were. By midmorning, the Thanksgiving snowstorm had pushed into Canada, and the skies had cleared for the first time in days. Merchants bustled about getting their stores decorated while the garden club was busy putting up the Christmas tree in the town commons. Everyone was in high spirits, enjoying the clear weather and anticipating the holiday festivities. At twilight, the lights all came on at once. They twinkled brightly in all the store windows, and the Norwegian spruce in the town common sparkled with hundreds of colored lights against the backdrop of the fresh snow that lay on the ground. The clear night sky was festooned with a myriad of bright stars, and the full moon cast its silver light across the white crystalline blanket that had covered Saint Basile for weeks. Carly and Scott caught up with each other just as the tree was lit. Almost a hundred people had gathered around it, and their exclamations of delight when the lights came on echoed through the cold air. Carly knelt down beside Silk, hugging him tightly. She looked up at Scott. "I didn't think it would be this beautiful. The whole town. So beautiful. Maybe I'll fall in love with snow again after all."

TWENTY-FIVE

The next two weeks were clear and mostly sunny. Some of the high-piled drifts had melted considerably, and people started to forget the barrage of bad weather that had recently descended on them. Carly hadn't seen Kate Malone since Thanksgiving Day, and while she had called and left messages a few times, Kate had never returned the calls. She and Scott tried to be together as often as they could while at the same time keeping a low profile when working. Carly was still concerned about what people would think, and she didn't want to be the subject of local gossip. The Malone family was the topic of conversation between them on many evenings over dinner. Scott thought that Carly was overreacting regarding her fears about Kate's safety, but she refused to change her mind, and he finally stopped chiding her about it.

Carly stopped at the market after work frequently, and one afternoon, she happened to see Smitty helping at one of the registers. There weren't many people in the place, so she went through his register to talk with him.

"Hey, Smitty. Nice to see you doing some work for a change," she joked.

"Aw, c'mon, Carly. Give me a break, will ya!"

"Just kidding," she replied. "Hey, I'm wondering if you've seen the Malones around town lately."

"I saw Kate drive into town a couple of weeks ago when the roads were good," Smitty said. "She stopped in here with Maura to pick up some groceries. I've been letting her run up a tab, but I gotta tell ya, it's getting pretty big. I'll let it go a bit longer. Maybe Sean will find some work."

"Do you think Kate and Maura looked okay, Smitty?" Carly asked.

"Well, she sure didn't take any time to socialize. Just did her shopping, all businesslike. She looked tired too, walking with her head down all the time, and covered up with a woolen scarf. Maura was awful quiet, but I guess they're okay, Carly. Kate sure seemed preoccupied. Not like her usual self. Why? Is something going on out there?" he asked.

"I'm worried about them, Smitty," Carly said. "I keep hoping I'll run into Kate in town, but so far, I think you're the only one who has seen her. I call her all the time, but she never returns my calls. I'm thinking that I might just take a run out there in the morning to see if everything is okay."

Carly finished gathering her groceries, telling Smitty she would let him know if she found out anything, then headed out to her car. She decided to stop at the library on the way home to rent a few movies. She drove the truck to the end of Main Street, where the library shared space with some of the town offices. Just as she was pulling into a parking space in front of the building, Kate Malone pulled in behind her in Sean's white truck. Carly waited until Kate got out of the truck before she got out of her own truck to say hello. Silk spotted Maura right away, barking loudly to get her attention. Kate turned around when she heard the dog, looking surprised to see Carly, almost embarrassed. Carly walked over to Kate and gave her a quick hug.

"Kate, I've been calling you for days," Carly said. "Haven't you been getting my messages? I was beginning to think that either you were mad at me or that you had left town!"

Kate looked at Carly with a puzzled expression.

"I haven't seen any messages from you, Carly. Sean hasn't mentioned any either. Are you sure you are calling the right number? I've been in and out a lot, but I am sure Sean would have told me that you called." Carly knew she was dialing the correct number because she was getting the Malone's message on the answering machine. She decided not to push the issue, realizing that Sean wasn't letting Kate know about the calls.

"You may be right, Kate," she said. "I'll check the number again when I get home." Kate was fidgeting with her coat and looked anxious to get away from Carly.

"Okay. Well, nice to see you, Carly. Gotta run," Kate told her as she turned to start up the stairs. She had pulled the woolen scarf over her face, covering it to just under her nose. Maura stood clinging to Kate's coat, Raggedy Ann tucked under her tiny arm, not looking at Carly at all. Carly noticed a hint of a bruise under Kate's right eye, just a shadow, but enough to make her scrutinize her friend's face for other marks. She tried to make conversation with Maura, but the little girl seemed unwilling to say anything more than a quiet hello. After a minute of strained silence, Kate made another dismissive comment about being in a hurry and then started up the steps of the library quickly. Maura followed her, and neither one of them looked back or waved good-bye. Carly stood watching them from the bottom of the granite stairs, puzzled by Kate's dismissive behavior and concerned about the marks on her face.

She watched Kate trudge up the stone steps, hunched into the wind, and was reminded of the old women in Renaissance oil paintings, going to market all shrouded up in their black shawls. Kate's usual exuberance was gone, replaced by an uncharacteristic caution. Unnerved by the surprise meeting, Carly decided against any movie rentals that day and got back in the truck to head for home. Scott was joining her for dinner, and she was anxious to tell him about this strange meeting.

It was already dark by the time Carly got home. Scott arrived at five thirty and helped her set the table and start dinner. He lit a fire, and they sat on the couch, enjoying a glass of wine. "You'll never guess who I ran into today," Carly said. "Kate and Maura. Ran into them at the library."

"Did you get a chance to talk to her?"

"For about one minute. She didn't want to stop and chat at all, and Maura just hid behind her coat. Kate was all shrouded up with a scarf wrapped around her face, almost covering her eyes. She was bruised around the eye, Scott. I didn't mention it to her, but she definitely had a shiner. That husband of hers probably gave it to her."

"Not much anyone can do about it, Carly," he said. "We could step in at some point, but we have to have proof of a problem, and Kate would have to be willing to press charges on Sean. My guess is that's probably not going to happen."

"I know. You're right. But I just wish there was something I could do. I have the feeling that there is going to be disaster at Lakeview Farm in the not-too-distant future, and I would feel horrible if I didn't try to do something to prevent it," Carly said.

"Don't you think Kate would tell you if she needed help?" Scott asked.

"No, I don't think she would. She's too scared. And besides, I get the feeling that she is avoiding me these days because she knows that I know that something is not right in that house. I'll keep trying to catch up with her, but I don't think it's going to do any good. I'm pretty certain now that Sean is not telling her when I leave a message. And I am positive that he is physically abusing both Kate and Maura. But as you say, there's not a damned thing we can do about it without proof."

"Carly, the only thing we can do right now is keep a watch on things out there. If we come up with anything, anything at all that would allow us to move on Sean, then I promise you we will do just that. For now all we can do is be vigilant."

The Malones were slowly coming apart at the seams, and no one on the outside knew what was happening. Sean hadn't worked in weeks and the small salary that Kate made at the hospital barely kept them afloat. They were almost completely isolated from their neighbors because of the weather and Kate was afraid to call Carly for fear that Sean would find out and erupt into one of his tantrums. She felt as if she were walking on eggshells whenever she was around him, and Maura had learned to avoid him entirely. Kate tried to talk to him but her attempts infuriated him. He had taken to pushing her around, even hitting her on occasion, accusing her of nagging at him all the time. Sean was a loaded gun, and Kate was trying desperately not to pull the trigger.

TWENTY-SIX

Saint Basile started to return to its normal routines as the weather continued its storm-free pattern. The town's merchants were enjoying the fruits of a brisk holiday business, and people's normal activities resumed completely. Carly's earlier worries about the weather grew more distant with each sunny day. She continued to call Kate, and her calls continued to go unanswered. She finally stopped leaving messages.

About a week before Christmas, Carly was in the diner waiting for Scott to join her for lunch. Callie Jensen walked in and spotted Carly at the counter. She waved as she walked toward the counter to grab the stool next to Carly. Callie was a senior manager at the First Trust Bank and knew everyone in town and their business. She was known as the town gossipmonger, but Carly liked her and always enjoyed catching up on the local "dirt." They exchanged pleasantries before Carly decided to ask her if the Malones had been into the bank recently. She was particularly interested in knowing about Sean and made sure that her tone of voice was nonchalant.

"Has Sean come into the bank lately, Callie? I've been trying to reach Kate and wonder if maybe they've gone on vacation or something."

"I haven't seen either of them lately," Callie replied. "But Eve Barton says she sees him pass her house every morning, like he was off to some job or something. Doesn't come home until after dark most days. Come to think of it. I do see him here around lunchtime once in a while. Says a quick hello, but that's about it. He grabs a sandwich and a coffee, maybe reads a few pages of the sports section, then gets in his truck and heads out. I don't think I've said two sentences to him in months."

"What about Kate and Maura? Have you seen them at all?"

"Not since just before Thanksgiving. But I did hear that Kate quit her job at the hospital. Everyone was really surprised, especially since Sean has been out of work. She just upped and gave her notice right after Thanksgiving and then walked out. Left them high and dry. Pissed off the nursing supervisor, I heard."

Carly was shocked to hear that Kate had left her job, but she decided to forego any further conversation with Callie about the Malones. Instead, she decided to call Kate again as soon as she got back to the office, hoping that she would be able to speak with her this time. Scott finally showed up and took the stool on Carly's other side. Carly was anxious to get back to the office and call Kate.

"I have to get going. Got some stuff to do back at the office. Wish I could stay and visit a while longer, but I can't."

She finished her sandwich quickly and caught the waitress's attention to bring the check. "I'll leave you two to trade some gossip while I'm gone. Just don't talk about me!"

Scott shot her a dirty look, not happy being left there alone to listen to Callie. Carly winked at him and headed out the door.

She called the Malones' number three or four times that afternoon, each time getting the answering machine message and leaving several messages, asking Kate to return the call. She never got a response. When Scott came back from lunch, Carly repeated what Callie had told her about Kate quitting her job.

He was surprised by the news as well.

"That's a shock," he said. "Now they're both out of work. I can't believe she quit the hospital! What are they going to do for money now?" he wondered aloud.

"I don't know, Scott, but I still can't get a response from her. I'm going to keep trying, but if it goes on much longer, I am going to go out there to check on them."

The weather forecasts started to turn ugly a couple of days before Christmas. The forecasters predicted a small snowstorm, but it turned into a multiday event. Carly and Scott planned to spend Christmas at her place, and they picked up a beautiful Norwegian spruce tree and some assorted lights and ornaments from the gift shop in town. Carly called her mother, inviting her for the last time to come and spend Christmas with her. Hannah declined the invitation, blaming George for not wanting to travel.

"Dear, we would love to come," she told Carly. "But your father just refuses to drive that far on a holiday, and he is worried about getting stuck in bad weather. You probably don't have room in that small place anyway for us, and I would hate to spend the nights in some dingy little country motel. Why don't you come here, Carly? We could invite Rachel and her family and some of our neighbors. We'd have a good time like the old days, dear."

"Mother, you know I can't do that. I have to work the day after Christmas. Tell Dad that I'm sorry that you won't be coming up. I'll call you on Christmas Day."

She hung up, resigning herself to the fact that her parents really didn't care to spend the holiday with her. Scott saw her disappointment.

"Carly, don't worry. We'll have a good time ourselves. They'll come around at some point, and in the meantime, there is nothing you can do to fix the situation anyway. C'mon, let's start putting the tree up."

They spent the remainder of the evening decorating the tree and the house and then settled back in front of the fireplace, listening to Christmas carols on the local radio station. Scott had not spent another night with Carly since the night of the ham and bean supper. He had wanted to, but she never extended another invitation and seemed to want to avoid the subject entirely. He was pretty sure that he hadn't done anything wrong and that her avoidance was simply an indication that she wasn't ready for a serious commitment. He hoped that she might change her mind on Christmas Day.

It started snowing again on Christmas Eve, and the storm lasted all through Christmas Day. The already-white Christmas was made whiter by another twenty inches of new snow. Carly called her parents just as she promised, but her father stubbornly refused to come to the phone. She kept the conversation brief and pleasant, although it was her mother who did most of the talking as usual.

She and Scott exchanged the few presents they bought for each other, and then when the roads were partially cleared, they walked with Silk to the center of town, enjoying the quiet peace of the late afternoon. A few people were out with their kids, pulling them on new sleds or watching them maneuver the snow-covered streets with their cross-country skis. They walked around the town common, unleashing Silk to let him run free for a while and then headed back to Carly's place to fix their Christmas dinner.

Carly made one last attempt to reach Kate and once again found herself talking to the answering machine.

Scott was standing beside Carly helping with the dishes when he suddenly turned to face her.

"Carly, I have to say this now before I lose my courage," he said. "I've fallen in love with you."

She started to respond back, but he put his finger to her lips so that she would be quiet.

"You don't have to say anything or even do anything. I don't expect you to, but I needed to tell you how I feel."

Scott's announcement was not really a surprise to Carly, but she hadn't expected him to verbalize it so soon. She was not sure how she felt about him. There were still some lingering feelings of guilt whenever they were together, and she couldn't help thinking that she was betraying Rob or at least betraying his memory. She knew that this was probably foolish, but she couldn't help it. Scott was wonderful to her, and she loved being with him. She was just not sure if she was in love with him. He knew that she was ambivalent and was willing to wait and let things work themselves out. She had been through a terrible tragedy, and he knew it would take time for her to heal.

Scott's hopes for spending Christmas night with Carly never materialized. They enjoyed the evening together, and when he began to make subtle comments about having to get home, she made no attempt to dissuade him from leaving. He left around midnight, and as he was about to open the door, part of her wanted to pull him back in and ask him to stay, but the other part told her to let him go. She walked him to the door and kissed him goodnight, wishing him a merry Christmas as he walked out. He stood on the sidewalk, wishing that the evening had ended differently. Carly was the first woman he had met since his wife's death that made him feel whole again, and he wondered if she would ever feel the same way about him.

TWENTY-SEVEN

The run of stormy weather forced Saint Basile to cancel some of its normal holiday festivals, but the town still managed to hold its annual New Year's Day bonfire and potluck supper. It snowed off and on all day on January 1, but despite the stormy day, the men were able to stack up dozens of old wooden pallets for the bonfire, and the women worked all morning and afternoon in the town hall kitchen, preparing their specialty recipes for the potluck supper that night. Even Carly made a contribution by sharing a big Crock-Pot filled with her mother's "famous" Boston baked beans recipe.

To Carly's surprise, the Malones showed up for all the New Year's Day events. Carly was helping some children with a snowman when she spotted them across the street from her and waved and shouted to get their attention, but Kate quickly turned away, with Sean walking ahead of her. Carly knew that Kate had seen her, but she didn't understand why Kate purposely snubbed her. Maura was tucked in closely to Kate, almost wrapped in her mother's long woolen coat, just like the day at the library. Carly was hurt that Kate had ignored her, and she stood staring at the Malones as they made their way through the crowd lined up along the curb.

Jenn Cassidy, Kate's supervisor at the hospital, was standing beside Carly and saw what had happened.

"Don't take it personally, Carly," Jenn said, giving Carly a little shoulder hug. "Kate has been acting like that since before she quit her job. Everyone is wondering what the heck has happened to her. She's been like that with everyone for quite a while now."

"What do you think is going on with her, Jenn?" Carly asked.

"I have no idea, Carly. Wish I did. She started coming in late or missing staff meetings. I asked her a couple of times if things were okay at home, but she would just clam up on me or change the subject. Sean's not working, so I can't imagine why she would give up her job like that."

Carly admitted that it was a pretty strange thing to do.

"A lot of us have been wondering if she's sick. What do you think, Carly?" Jenn asked.

"The thought crossed my mind, too, Jenn. I just saw her a while back and thought she looked awful. Didn't want to spend time talking with me either. I haven't been able to speak with her since Thanksgiving except for one time when I met her in front of the library," Carly replied. "You saw what just happened. Almost like the day at the library. She seems to be purposely avoiding me."

"I don't think it's just you, Carly," Jenn said. "She's been that way with all of us lately."

The two women chatted a bit more, and Jenn finally wandered off to talk to some friends from the hospital. Carly had the cold-all-over feeling again as she watched Jenn walk off. She looked across the crowd, trying to see if the Malones were still there, but they had disappeared. She felt chilled to the bone all of a sudden, and she wrapped her jacket around her tightly and pulled the hood up over her head, trying to get warm. Scott saw her standing alone, shivering, and walked over to her.

"What's the matter, Carly?" he asked. "You look like you just saw a ghost."

"I think I did, Scott. I think I just saw Kate Malone's ghost."

TWENTY-EIGHT

The Malones got home from the New Year's Day events around seven o'clock. It had been a long day, and Maura was tired and whining about everything. Kate felt badly about ignoring Carly earlier in the day, but Sean had been in such a vile mood that she thought it best to just keep walking, pretending that she hadn't seen Carly at all. Kate got Maura into bed right after supper, and when she came back downstairs, she tried to engage Sean in conversation.

"Sean, we need to talk. Would you shut that TV off for a minute?"

"I don't want to talk right now. Can't you see I'm watching the game? Kate, gimme a break, will ya! It's been a long day, and I'm tired."

Kate, bristling with anger, walked over to the TV and turned it off, then she stood in front of it with her arms folded across her chest.

"You *are* going to talk to me, Sean, and you're going to do it right now! We can't go on like this," she told him. He shifted uneasily in his chair, unaccustomed to having Kate challenge him. "I can't take your sour moods any more. You're impossible to live with, and I don't see things getting any better. I'm taking Maura and going to stay with my mother for a while. Maura is so afraid of you these days. Don't you even notice that she avoids you totally? You treat me like dirt, and I'm not going to take that abuse anymore from you. And I'm not going to let you hit me anymore either. I've had enough."

She was shaking with fear and anger, but she went on, scolding about the animals. "And you can't leave those poor animals out there without food, Sean. For heaven's sake, get them some hay or something. They're starving. Sell something if you have to, but buy them some feed or sell them. They're going to die if you don't do something."

Sean listened, glaring sullenly at her, then got up from the recliner chair and grabbed her by both arms, hurting her as he squeezed.

"You listen to me, you spoiled Irish brat. You aren't going anywhere, and you're not taking my kid anywhere either. Your place is here, understand? And as far as those animals are concerned, they cost too much to keep anyway. They can starve to death for all I care."

He had released her arms and grabbed her by the shoulders, shaking her as he talked. Kate tried to escape, but he moved to her side and caught her head and neck in the crook of his elbow, putting a viselike pressure on her.

"You're a rotten human being, Sean, and I'm leaving you, and Maura is coming with me. I should have listened to my sister. She was right about you. You're no good."

He pulled her head in tightly against his chest.

"I'll kill you, Kate, if you try to leave me. I promise you, I will kill you."

He pushed her away, shoving her to the floor and then kicked her in the side before he stomped out of the family room and into the kitchen. Kate heard him opening another beer and knew that it would only make things worse. She was crying and afraid to make another sound, but she managed to get herself up quietly and move toward the stairs to be out of his way. Maura had heard them fighting, and Kate found her standing at the top of the stairs, crying, with her Raggedy Ann doll under her arm.

"It's okay, baby. It's okay. Come with Mama. I'll read you a story."

Kate went up to the top of the stairs and picked up Maura and her doll and brought her back to her bedroom.

While she was tucking Maura into her bed, the little girl looked up at her with teary eyes. "What's wrong with Daddy, Mama? He is so mad all the time. I don't like him anymore, and he scares me."

"I don't know, honey. Don't be scared. Daddy loves us. He just gets upset because he can't find work these days. It will get better. Honest. Now settle down, and I'll read a story to you, okay?"

Kate steadied her voice as she read, and after a few minutes, Maura drifted off to sleep. She closed Maura's bedroom door and went quietly into the master's bedroom. She sat in the big armchair by the window, wrapping herself in the shawl that was draped over the back of the chair. The snow had let up, and she sat staring out at the pristine expanse of the snow-covered pasture behind the house. A few random flakes drifted by the window, glittering in the wash of silver moonlight. She had made up her mind. She would leave at dawn while Sean was still asleep. She quietly pulled a small overnight suitcase from the shelf in the closet and threw some clothing into it, just enough for a few days. Then she went into Maura's room and grabbed a few of her things, adding them to the messy pile in the suitcase. She latched it up and tucked it under Maura's bed then went back to her own room to take a shower and go to bed herself. Sean finally came upstairs, weaving his way into the bedroom. He collapsed, drunk, on the bed beside her, stinking of stale beer. She waited until he was asleep and then went downstairs to sit on the family room sofa. She didn't sleep at all that night.

Just before sunrise, she woke Maura to get her dressed.

"Maura, don't make any noise," she said. "We don't want to wake Daddy up."

"Where are we going, Mama? I don't want to go out right now."

"We're going to Grammy's house, and we have to leave early, honey. C'mon now. Let me get you dressed."

"I want Raggedy, Mama. She has to come with me," Maura whined.

Kate was starting to get impatient, wanting to get out of the house before daybreak.

"Okay, okay. Take Raggedy. Just hurry up and come with me now."

Still half-asleep, Maura followed Kate quietly down the stairs. Kate had the suitcase and grabbed the keys to her SUV from the hallway table. It was frigid outside. She could hear a couple of the animals calling from the barn and wished that she could feed them some little thing, but there was no feed.

She opened the garage door quietly, and she and Maura got into the front seat of the SUV. The engine wouldn't kick over. She tried again and then again, finally flooding it.

Sean was awakened by the sounds in the garage, and seeing that Kate was not in bed, he threw on his jeans and raced downstairs and out the back door. Kate saw him come out the kitchen door. She grabbed Maura and got her out of the vehicle and onto the driveway. Suitcase in one hand, child in the other, she tried to push her way through the deep snow. She made it to the edge of the driveway when she heard Sean's truck start up. The headlights were blinding as the truck headed toward them, plowing snow aside as it moved forward. Fear rose like bile in her throat and mouth, and she ran screaming, with Maura holding her hand until she reached the snowdrift at the edge of the street. She looked back just as the huge blade of the plow bore down on her and her little girl.

TWENTY-NINE

When the last of the New Year's Day crowd had gone home, Carly stayed with Scott and some of the DPW crew to make sure that there were no burning embers left lying around from the fireworks display or the bonfire. By 7:00 p.m., the town commons had been cleaned up, and Carly headed for home. Scott promised to join her later after he took care of a few things at his place. It had snowed steadily all day, and the roads were icing up as the temperature dropped. Carly was glad that she was within walking distance of the commons and didn't have to drive on the icy roadways. She and Silk walked at a brisk pace, anxious to get out of the cold.

When she got home, she fed Silk and heated up some leftovers for her own supper. She fixed some herbal tea and settled into the old armchair to watch the remains of the big bowl games. When the games ended, she gave Kate a call, hoping to wish her a Happy New Year. No answer, just the answering machine.

She hung up without leaving a message and headed to the bedroom, thinking that she would take a short nap. Scott hadn't arrived yet, and she was suddenly feeling very tired. She had not been able to get warm since the afternoon, and she threw an extra quilt over the goose down comforter already on the bed, hoping to ward off some of the chill. It was still snowing hard, and she stared from her bed at the white veil that had covered the windowpanes in her room. She slipped off into an uneasy sleep.

The snow was stinging her face, and she huddled down at the doorstep, still pounding at the door for Sean to open it and let her in. She was shivering and crying at the same time. Her tears were freezing as they fell, forming huge ice drops on her cheeks. She forced herself to stand up, and when she looked into the kitchen again, Sean and Kate were gone, and the room was dark except for a small nightlight on the stove. Raggedy Ann sat propped up on one of the kitchen chairs, her embroidered smile twisted into a hideous grin, her black button eyes gone, leaving only a cross stitch of thread where they had been sewn to her face.

She pushed hard against the door until it gave in to her weight and poured her into the room in a swirl of wet snow. The groaning wind enveloped the house. She called into the darkness, but the only sound she heard back was the creaking of the old house timbers as they strained against the onslaught of the storm. The black crows were in the kitchen, walking back and forth across the hard countertop at the sink, their talons clicking against the stone. They watched her with cold eyes, ruffling their wing feathers each time she moved, protesting her intrusion into the house.

She was awakened by Scott shaking her, trying to wake her up. She sat up and stared at him for a minute, disoriented. Her hair was damp with perspiration, and the bedding was rumpled into a knot of sheets and down comforters. He climbed into bed with her, holding her head against his chest. Neither one of them said a word until Scott finally broke the silence.

"How bad was it this time, Carly?" he asked.

"Bad. Really bad," she said.

"They are getting worse, Scott, and they're so vivid! It's strange, but they seem to continue on where the last one left off, and they are always about the Malones and a storm, and…I don't know, Scott, I think maybe they are a premonition of something awful going to happen there. I can't seem to pick them apart enough to figure out what they mean."

"What do you *think* they mean?" he asked.

"If you really want to know, I think they mean that Sean is going to do something terrible to Kate and maybe Maura. I've felt this for a long time. He's dangerous, Scott, and I've thought for a while that he's been ready to explode."

"I know you have, Carly, but we have nothing of any substance to be certain about him. Yeah, I know he has probably been physically abusive, but Kate is a smart woman, and I just don't think she would put up with that kind of treatment, do you?"

"I think she feels trapped, Scott, and I think she is worried about Maura as well. Sometimes women put up with that abuse when they have kids. You know that. I'm sure you've seen it plenty of times."

"Yeah, you may be right, but until we have something tangible, Carly, there's not much we can do. I've told you that before."

"I know, I know, but these nightmares mean something, Scott. I'm not crazy. I know they do, and I'm worried because I feel as though our hands are so tied. I'll never forgive myself if something does happen, and we just sat here and did nothing to prevent it."

THIRTY

A major blizzard hit northern Vermont on January 3, dumping record amounts of snow on the lake region. The storm was fueled by lake-effect winds and temperatures, and it continued to pummel Saint Basile for four days. Captain McIntyre instructed Scott to call up the National Guard to bring in some emergency food supplies, water, and fuel by helicopter because the normal delivery trucks just couldn't seem to make it through during the bad weather. Carly and Scott were working almost around the clock, too exhausted to do anything but sleep when they had free time. The weather had transformed everything. Streets filled up with snow as quickly as they got plowed out, and the equipment couldn't stay ahead of it. Forecasters were baffled by the storm's pattern, and their daily predictions were the same: more snow. Almost every tree and shrub was laden down with heavy snow and ice, some with boughs touching the ground and frozen in place. Huge snow banks lined the narrow streets and roads as the plows worked nonstop trying to keep the roads passable.

By the end of the first week in January, everything in Saint Basile came to a halt. Schools were closed until further notice, merchants boarded up the shops, and all that remained open was Smitty's grocery store, the pharmacy, the fire and police station, and the hospital. One gas station at the outskirts of town stayed open off and on, but nobody was driving anywhere, and eventually that closed as well.

Carly's bad dreams started to come on a nightly schedule, disrupting what little sleep she was able to get. Scott urged her to seek medical attention, but she refused, telling him that it was just a passing problem, but she was more concerned about it than she let on to him. Every night, the dreams jolted her awake, and she found herself in cold sweats with a racing heartbeat. She was cold all the time and couldn't get warm no matter how many layers of clothing she wore. Scott had used more than half of the winter supply of cordwood, trying to keep the woodstove burning hot for her when they were in the office.

To make matters worse that week, Jack McIntyre was forced into retirement due to his chronic health condition, leaving Carly and Scott to manage the police department on their own. They had been doing most of the work anyway, but Jack at least had been able to cover for them in the office once in a while or take on some of the extra paperwork. They scrambled to get a handle on all the administrative work that the captain had to do, and along with trying to help the townspeople get through their various weather disasters, there was not much downtime for either of them. This, along with sleepless nights, put Carly on edge, and she and Scott began to argue with each other over insignificant things, which cooled their relationship to the point where they only saw each other at work. Carly knew it was her fault that they had drifted apart, but she felt powerless to repair the damage. Scott decided to let things lay quiet for a while. He was frustrated with the situation but knew that Carly was the only one who could fix it.

Many of the townspeople were isolated by the storm, and everyone took turns checking on those families on the outskirts of town as a daily task. Carly had not spoken with Kate for a couple of weeks, but she had gone by the Malones' place a few times, and everything seemed to be in order. There were always some lights on in the house and signs of footpaths between the house and the barn. The animals were never out, but then no one had their livestock out in the bad weather, so she didn't think much more about it.

Smitty made a heroic effort to get out to people with food and supplies. He had a solid delivery truck and tried to make a daily run with groceries that had been ordered over the phone.

He caught up with Carly one morning before he headed out and mentioned that he was worried about the Malones.

"Honestly, Carly," he said, "I haven't seen Kate or Sean in weeks. She used to come in every Thursday and pick up groceries. Ain't been here since New Year's. Ain't even called in an order. Wonder if they're okay up there."

"I tried to check on them yesterday, Smitty," she told him.

"Half the driveway was plowed, and there were some fresh tire tracks running to the street. A few lights were on upstairs, but I didn't see any real signs of movement out there. It almost looked like they had gone off someplace. The place looked unusually quiet, especially around the barn area. I've been calling, but Kate never gets back to me. Maybe I should just go up there unannounced and see what the hell is going on, especially since the storm coming looks pretty bad."

Carly planned to drive out to Lakeview Farm as soon as the weather let up and she could grab some free time. The snow and bitter cold became a daily constant. Stinging winds howled across the frozen lake, and the open fields sent tornadoes of light snow swirling across the flat surfaces. There was not a recognizable landmark anywhere. The power company had managed to keep electricity on for three of the four days, but on the fourth day, everything went down. The cell phones were the only means of communication for the police department, and Carly and Scott tried to keep them charged in the truck. Everything was immobilized, and there wasn't a sign of life in the town until the snow finally stopped and the DPW managed to get out and get a consistent cleanup going. Smitty was deluged with grocery orders and quickly ran out of the meager store of supplies he had managed to muster up before the storm. There were still some emergency supplies left from the National Guard deliveries, but those went quickly as well.

When the phones came back on, some of the women started making calls around, checking on families that hadn't yet surfaced, finding most of them just busy trying to dig themselves out. Emily Turner called the Malone place and spoke to Sean, but not Kate. Sean told her they were all okay but that Kate and Maura had come down with the flu and were in bed. He assured Emily that all was well and not to worry. Emily, assuming that the Malones were all right, didn't let anyone know she had talked with Sean until a few days later.

THIRTY-ONE

After the blizzard, everybody bent their backs to the shovels, trying to dig themselves out. The business of living went on, but it was pale and silent like the snow that had come in sideways and filled the world's holes with its icy mortar. Snowdrifts were piled higher than ten feet in some locations, and the little bit that the sun had melted just froze over during the cold nights. Moving about was a treacherous business. School reopened a week after the blizzard, and by then, most activity was back to normal. Carly didn't know it at the time, but Maura Malone never showed up for the first day back to school or for any of the days after that. Harry Mitchell, the principal, kept calling the house, but he always got a busy signal. He never sent someone out to check on the Malone family, and he never called anyone else to voice his concern. Carly wanted to check on the Malones herself, but she feared that a visit from her might infuriate Sean and put Kate and Maura at risk. She tried calling several times, but like Harry Mitchell, she also got constant busy signals.

The day after the school reopened, Carly was parked on Main Street, watching for the afternoon parade of school buses. Scott was back at the office. Silk was with her, sitting quietly in the back seat. He suddenly jumped to the front of the cab, barking wildly. Carly tried to quiet him and then saw what had agitated him. There was a horse staggering aimlessly down the center of the street. Carly recognized the animal as Rocky, the Malones' draft horse. The animal was over seventeen hands high and had been broad in the beam and chest when she had first seen him. Carly watched him stumble along the road, appalled at his frail appearance. He was thin and wasted, with dirt and manure clinging to him everywhere, and he was so lame that he was barely able to lift one foot ahead of another to keep moving. She suspected that he had broken out of his stall in the barn because she could see slivers of slat board stuck here and there in his halter and in his tangled mane. His thick tail was matted, and his hooves were overgrown and caked with balls of frozen snow. Carly subdued Silk's barking and grabbed some rope from the back seat. She let Silk out of the truck, and with him by her side, they walked quietly up to the horse. Carly talked softly to Rocky as they approached.

"Don't be afraid, Rocky. We aren't going to hurt you."

The horse tried to keep moving forward, but he was in shock and finally stood still, trembling with pain, his huge head lowered almost to the ground, his eyes half closed and dull. Carly continued to talk softly to him as she moved closer so that she could get the rope tied to his halter. Silk sensed something was terribly wrong and kept nudging his nose at Rocky's front legs, trying to get him to move. Carly managed to grab the leather halter and tie the rope through the chin ring, talking to the horse all the while. Holding him tightly by the halter, she took her cell phone from her pocket and called Dr. Evert, the county vet. It seemed to take forever for him to answer the phone, and Carly became more anxious with each ring.

"Hello, this is Donald Evert. May I help you?"

"Doc, this is Carly Richardson. I need your help with a pretty sick horse that wandered into town. I have him in hand now. It's Sean Malone's draft horse, Rocky."

Briefing him as best she could about the situation, Carly told him that Rocky's condition seemed pretty desperate. As soon as she ended the call, she paged Scott. He called her back instantly.

"What's going on, Carly?"

"Oh, Scott. The Malone's draft horse just wandered into town, half dead. The poor thing. I just called the vet to come and get him. Can you get down to lower Main Street? That's where we are. I have the horse in hand now," she told him.

"I'll be right there, Carly. On my way now," he replied.

Within five minutes, both Scott and the vet arrived. Doc Evert looked Rocky over, checking his gums for anemia and his heart for rapid beat. He ran his hands along the horse's sides and flanks, feeling the rib cage and pelvic bones pressed tightly against the skin with no insulating fat between.

"Carly, this is a dangerously sick animal. He's malnourished for sure and looks like he may have foundered, which is why he can't walk well. I need to get him back to the clinic to see if there is something we can do for him. I'm not very hopeful, and I have a feeling he may not make it through the night. If he's foundered too badly, I may have to put him down. Let's load him onto the trailer and say a little prayer that we can fix this."

He and Scott loaded Rocky into the vehicle and covered him with blankets while Carly, still holding Silk on a leash, looked on sadly. "We'll rig him up with some IVs when we get to the clinic and see what we can do. I suspect that the damage may be too much too repair. I'll call you tomorrow. Has anyone contacted Sean about this?"

"Not yet, Doc. Haven't had time," Carly replied.

"I'll call him when I get back, Carly. Don't worry about it."

With that, the vet closed up the rear of the trailer and headed the truck back to his veterinary clinic just outside town.

Scott walked over to Carly and put his arm around her shoulders. Neither of them spoke, but the recent strain in their relationship eased a little with that simple gesture.

"I locked the office up, Carly. Let me get you home," Scott said.

He pulled his own car over to the curb, leaving it there, and helped Carly and Silk into the truck. They were silent on the drive back to Carly's condo. Scott grabbed Carly's gloved hand, giving it a gentle squeeze. She kept looking out the passenger window, but she knew that they were all right with each other again.

The forecast called for more snow throughout the night and into the next morning, the tail end of the storm that had just paralyzed the small town. The roads were already treacherous, and Scott had to maneuver the truck carefully around the drifting snow in the streets. By the time they reached her place, Carly was physically and mentally exhausted. Scott fixed some tea for her and fed Silk and let him out for a quick run.

"Carly, why don't you go find a good movie to watch. I'll clean up here," Scott told her.

"I was just thinking I might do that. I'll find something that we both will like," she said.

By the time he let the dog back in, Carly was already stretched out on her living room sofa. The snow was still coming down heavy and wet, and it pelted against the building like small hammers, trying to break through the brick. The sky had turned an eerie cold yellow color, and it seemed as if the sun had been weakened to try to break through the gray barrier of clouds. Carly stared out the window for a while as she sipped her tea, trying to put the day's events behind her, but instead, her mind flooded with remnants of the nightmares she had been having.

"Carly, are you going to be okay?" Scott asked. "I have to go back to the office and close up."

"I'll be fine," she told him. "Don't worry. I'm going to bed right after you leave."

"Do you want me to come back?" he asked, hopeful that she would say yes.

"No, Scott. Not tonight if you don't mind. It's been a horrible day, and I'm exhausted. Honestly, I'm fine. Just lock up after you, and I'll see you in the morning."

He leaned over the sofa and kissed her gently.

"Okay, but you'd better call me if you need anything," he said.

Carly shut off the lights once Scott had left the driveway and headed for the bedroom and what she hoped would be a good night's sleep. She fell asleep quickly, finding herself in the empty house, standing motionless in the dark kitchen, staring at the eyeless doll in the chair. The doll had been carefully arranged there. Its left arm rested in its lap, pointing toward the barn. The other arm was holding the white apron aside so that the bright blue calico dress was in full view. She thought the doll's mouth was moving, and she moved closer, trying to see, but the embroidered mouth settled back into a silent and sinister grin. Two crows perched on the back of the chair were pulling at the doll's red yarn hair, grabbing bits in their beaks and dropping them to the floor. They cackled at each other loudly as they ripped at the bright yarn, leaving bare spots on the doll's cloth head.

The strident ring of the alarm clock woke her, but she just lay in bed, freezing under her down comforters, waiting for the first rays of morning sun to light up her east-facing bedroom window.

Doc Evert called her around seven to tell her that he had found Rocky dead in the clinic stall.

"Couldn't save him, Carly. He was just too far gone. Couldn't reach anyone at the Malone place either. Just kept getting a busy signal all night," he said. "I think you probably need to get out there and let them know what has happened."

Carly thanked him for letting her know and immediately called Scott.

"Scott, Rocky died last night," she told him. "We need to get out to the Malone place right away. You took the truck last night, so will you come and get me?"

"I'll be there in a few minutes, Carly. Just sit tight."

She threw on her uniform, grabbed her hat and revolver, and headed out the door when Scott arrived. They made their way to Lakeview Farm, driving slowly over the rutted road. The snow had stopped although the sky was still bloated with dark bulging clouds. The plows had put the main road in fair condition, but the secondary roads were still in pretty bad shape with ice pack hidden under the sand and coarse salt. The jagged edge of the cold air cut through their layers of clothing when they started out, and Carly jacked up the heat in the truck, trying to chase off the clinging chill. When they got to Lakeview Farm, Scott had to stop the truck about a quarter of the way up the drive because it was impassable from that point. The tire tracks and plow marks Carly had seen a few days ago were still slightly visible, but covered over now with the new snowfall. There were no signs of fresh tire tracks anywhere else. The front walk to the house was still covered with heavy snowpack, and several large drifts had all but covered the front windows. All the window shades were drawn on the second level, and there was no smoke coming from the furnace chimney or the fireplace, a sure sign that the heat was not on in the place. This time, there were no lights.

THIRTY-TWO

The Malone's mailbox looked as if it would overflow with envelopes and newspaper flyers. Carly grabbed what she could fit in a handful, glancing quickly at some of it. There were a few ominous-looking notices from the utility company and the oil company, along with another dozen envelopes that appeared to be bills. Carly felt an icy wave of fear wash over her.

"What do you make of this, Scott? This mail is at least a couple of weeks old. I didn't notice it the last time I came by. Do you think they just upped and left?"

"I don't know, but I don't like the look of things around here, I'll tell you that," he replied. "The house looks abandoned, and I'm more concerned that there are no signs of the animals having been out at all for a long time. Look over there at the paddock. Not disturbed one bit. You'd think there would at least be some furrows in the snow if they had been out."

They closed up the truck and headed up the long snow-covered driveway with the dog beside them. Carly looked over at the barn, surprised to see the main barn door wide open, but there were no signs of a shoveled path between it and the house. She could just about make out Rocky's labored trail in the snow, leading from the open barn door, across the small field in front of the barn, and out to the edge of the street. Icicles hung from the gutters of the barn, nearly touching the ground in some spots, imprisoning the building with crystal bars.

"Scott, look. The barn door is wide open. Sean never left that door open, especially in cold weather. And if Rocky really did break out, no telling what else we'll find in there."

It took them almost fifteen minutes to foot-plow themselves, waist deep in snow, up to the open barn door. Silk struggled to maneuver himself through the deep snow in order to stay up with them. By the time they all reached the barn, they were nearly exhausted from the sheer effort of moving through the deep drifts.

The barn was dark except for a little shaft of light coming in from the window above the hayloft. It took a minute for their eyes to adjust to the dimly lit building. Some birds fluttered excitedly up near the rafters, frightened by the intrusion. Their sudden racket startled Carly, and she froze in place when she realized that the noisy birds were crows. Probably the same pests that were hanging about the place all the time. They were the only signs of life in the whole place, and their rasping clatter assaulted the cold silence. Silk began to tremble, and he slung himself low, nose to the ground as if he were stalking prey. Carly knew he was frightened.

"It's okay, boy. Just a couple of noisy birds."

She patted his head a few times and walked forward with him toward the center of the barn. Scott had gone ahead of her, pointing the beams of his flashlight along the floor and up the walls of the building. When Carly's eyes finally adjusted to the darkness, she was able to identify shovels and manure rakes scattered around the barn floor and a wheelbarrow filled with shavings that were wedged up against the left side of the door opening. The whole place smelled foul, and sharp odors of must and decay filled her nostrils. She covered her nose and mouth with her scarf, trying to block out the horrific stench.

Carly could see the stall that Rocky had broken open. The door had been pushed out and lay flat in front of the large empty stall. She moved forward into the barn and found Scott standing motionless in front of two other smaller, stalls. The animals that had lived in those stalls were dead, their corpses frozen solid and stuck to the filthy ground around them.

"How could they have let this happen, Scott? How could anyone do this?"

She was holding Scott's arm, looking around in horror at the sight and smell of death everywhere. She struggled to process what she was seeing as she moved from stall to stall.

The scene repeated itself in every stall. Scott turned to her, his face distorted with anger.

"I'd like to put him in jail for letting these animals die like this. He could have called the humane society to come get them if he couldn't take care of them. What kind of person does this, Carly? There's not a scrap of feed anywhere in here. He just let these poor animals starve to death."

Carly looked at him and just shook her head. There were no words to express how she felt just then.

Carly knew they had to get to the house, and grabbing Scott by the hand, she turned to the barn door, stumbling over the scattered rakes as she rushed to get out. She let Silk off the leash, and he ran out of the barn, anxious to get away from it. Carly was gasping for breath as she exited, and Scott looked back in disbelief at what he has just seen. They moved with caution through the deep snow, finally reaching the landing at the entrance to the kitchen. The kitchen door was locked, with the curtains drawn across the glass. There was a sudden commotion of noise above the house, and Carly looked up to see a murder of crows circling the roof in a raucous convention and then landing one by one along the peak near the main chimney. They bobbed and weaved, moving their black bodies like tribal dancers, and as they moved, their cold yellow eyes followed every step that Scott and Carly took. Scott waved his arms and yelled at them until they dispersed noisily into the nearby trees.

Carly pushed the doorbell four or five times, knocked, pounded, and then just broke open one of the glass panes near the doorknob with the butt end of her service revolver as she announced their entry. They were there officially, and she wanted to make sure that their entrance was done properly. She stepped into the gloomy kitchen and moved forward cautiously across the room. Scott was behind her, his revolver ready in his hand. "Anyone here?" she called, stepping carefully across the tiled floor.

"Kate? Sean?"

No answer. The place was bitterly cold with only some fading light coming through the window. Dirty dishes were piled up in the sink and all over the small kitchen table. Carly whispered to Scott.

"Something's happened, Scott. Kate kept this place immaculate. She never would have left a mess like this."

The pipes had frozen and burst under the sink, leaving ice patches all over the kitchen floor. Carly tried several light switches with no success, realizing that the electricity had been shut off. The telephone dangled soundlessly from the wall, its dial tone silenced. Carly called out again to Sean and Kate. Still no answer. She and Scott left the kitchen and headed to the main entrance hall. The silence in the house was profound, broken only by the squeak of their wet boots on the polished wood floors and the click of Silk's nails as he walked beside them. The stairway to the second floor was in the family room and just back from the front door.

"Carly, let me go on ahead," Scott said. "You cover from behind and keep a watch on the hallway and the front door."

Scott called out again as he headed up the dark curved staircase, revolver still in hand and cocked.

"Anyone home? Sean, Kate?"

Nothing. Not a whisper. Silk stayed behind, running frantically from room to room downstairs, growling in deep, low rumbles with his nose to the cold floor.

The upstairs was darker than the lower level, and they had to raise the beams on their flashlights high in order to see the way clear. Their breath came in quick bursts of white vapor that hovered above them in the cold air. Carly's chest hurt from breathing in the cold, and her throat and mouth were dry from fear. Scott edged along the hallway in front of her, opening the bedroom doors as he approached each one. Every room was in chaos, with clothing strewn all over the floors, unmade beds, and overturned furniture in places. The bathroom, like the kitchen, had ice patches all over the floor, and they could see where the pipe had burst below the bathroom sink.

"This is a train wreck up here. Looks like someone went nuts and tore everything up," Scott whispered.

"I'm afraid for Kate and Maura, Scott. Something has happened to them. I know it. I just know it. I should have come out here. I let it go too long."

"Carly, we don't know anything yet, so don't go getting all upset with yourself over something you had no control over. C'mon, let's go back downstairs and check around outside. There's no one here," Scott said.

Carly kept her gun cocked at the ready as she headed back toward the staircase. The dog was waiting for them at the foot of the stairway. "C'mon, Silk, we've got to go outside," she whispered to him when she reached the bottom stair. They proceeded quietly through the family room, and when they reached the kitchen door, they moved as quickly as they could to get out of the house.

Once outside, they stood on the small landing outside the kitchen door, scanning the grounds for anything that might help explain what had happened.

"Carly, we should check the garage," Scott said. "Maybe the cars are still here."

The garage was separate from the house, set back between the barn and the south side of the house by about fifty feet. Scott got to the garage first and wiped the snow from one of the windows. They could see that Sean's pickup truck with the plow was gone, but Kate's Explorer was still there, and both the driver side and passenger side doors were wide open. It looked like the keys were still in the ignition.

"This explains the old tire tracks in the driveway," Carly muttered to Scott. "Someone took off in the truck right after the snow stopped. Let's see if we can find anything else."

Snow had piled up in high drifts along the back side of the house, making it almost impossible for them to move beyond the protruding corner of the wooden deck. No footprints were evident anywhere. The back deck was covered with snow halfway up the sliding doors that led to the kitchen, and there was no sign that anyone had tried entering or exiting the sliders. "Carly, we aren't going to find anything here. I think they must have taken off someplace. Let's head back to the office." Scott grabbed her arm, helping her as they started down the driveway.

They pushed through waist-deep snow, stumbling as they inched their way toward the road. The snow wrapped itself around their legs like some stray cat wanting to be touched. The drifts were high in some spots, over five feet, but in others, the wind had shirred the snow to bare ground. They were halfway down the driveway when Scott suddenly stopped. "Carly, I think I see something sticking up out of that snowdrift just beyond the mailbox." Carly looked at the high drift, and instantly saw what had caught Scott's eye. Protruding from the street side of the drift, and barely visible, was a small scrap of fabric, stuck in the snow and flapping merrily in the wind like a ship's ensign. Carly's heart was racing. She knew what was sticking out of that drift, and she didn't want to go any further.

THIRTY-THREE

Scott pushed forward toward the fluttering scrap of cloth while Carly plunged along behind him, trying to stay upright. When they reached the drift, they could see that the fabric was a blue calico with a lacey edging. Carly stared at it, then dropped to her knees and began digging frantically with her mittened hands, uncovering more of the cloth as she pushed the snow aside. The ice crust on the surface cut her, and blood stains formed on the palm sides of her white mittens.

"Scott, I know what this is! I know what it is! Help me, please," she cried out.

Scott, looking puzzled by her comment, got down beside her, and together they dug deeper into the icy snow. Carly managed to uncover a piece of fabric large enough to pull, and with Scott's help, she tugged at corners of the cloth to free it from the snowdrift. She had a sick feeling in the pit of her stomach, certain of what they would find at the end of the brightly patterned piece. A final hard pull released the snow from around the bit of fabric, and they stood side by side, staring down into the hole they had just made. Staring vacantly back at them with its black button eyes was Maura's Raggedy Ann doll, still clothed in a white apron and a lace-trimmed blue calico dress. The red embroidered mouth grinned at them as they worked to free the doll from the ice.

Carly tugged at the red-and-white striped cloth legs, releasing the doll from the snowpack, and underneath where the doll had lain, was the frozen body of Maura Malone, dressed in a pink snowsuit, blue eyes open, and like her doll, staring up at them from the icy grave.

Neither Scott nor Carly said a word to each other. As if on cue, the clouds delivered a burst of wet snow. Soft white flakes fluttered to the ground, dropping icy kisses on the dead little girl's pale cheeks. Carly and Scott were immobilized as they watched the new snow blanketing the little girl's already frozen body, fearing that another horror lay beneath the body of the child. Carly collapsed in a sitting position on the road, too stunned to speak, barely hearing Scott screaming at her to go with him to the barn and get the shovels. Silk howled beside them in long mournful calls as he dug frantically into the snowdrift, sending chunks of ice flying in all directions. Scott left Carly and headed back into the barn alone, grabbing the two large shovels that hung beside the open door. He moved back to the roadside quickly and handed Carly one of the shovels.

"Carly, get up. Dig. I need you to help me dig."

His tone got her attention, and she stood up and began to work beside him, digging carefully around the child's body. Together they removed Maura's small corpse from the drift and placed it on the ground beside the doll. Then digging cautiously around the area where Maura had lain, they uncovered the frozen remains of Kate Malone. Kate's face was bloodied, and her body was twisted in a grotesque position, suggesting that there were broken bones in her arms and legs. Like Maura, she was dressed in winter gear, and buried beside her was a small suitcase, which had burst open, revealing clothing that had been hastily thrown, unfolded, into the case.

Silk lay down beside Maura and put his head on her chest. He moved his body as close to the little girl as he could get as if he was trying to protect her from the surrounding cold. He whimpered as he lay there, looking up at Carly with his sad dark eyes.

THIRTY-FOUR

C arly and Scott placed the two bodies side by side, watching them slowly disappear under the shroud of new snowfall.

Carly was suddenly overcome by a rush of energy fueled by anger. She started pacing back and forth in the road as she spoke.

"Scott, we need to call the county medical examiner. Let's get back to the truck and get on the phone. We need to call the hospital and get an ambulance out here too. And the state troopers. We need to notify them right away."

Scott was surprised by her sudden "take-command mode," but he nodded in agreement, and they headed back for the truck, following the tracks they had made earlier. Carly tried to get Silk to go with her, but he remained beside Maura's body and wouldn't budge. The heavy snowfall made walking difficult, and it had created a whiteout situation, limiting visibility to a few feet.

Carly dialed the coroner's office, and Paul Reynolds picked up right away.

"Paul, it's Carly Richardson. Can you get out to Lakeview Farm immediately?" she stammered. "Scott and I have just found the bodies of Kate Malone and her daughter Maura. Hurry, please."

"I'll head out there right now, Carly. Give me some time. The roads aren't in very good condition," he answered.

"I know, Paul. Be careful, but get here as quickly as you can."

Paul Reynolds made it out to the Malone farm in about fifteen minutes, and just as he was heading up the drive, the hospital ambulance pulled in behind him, lights still flashing and sirens blaring. Paul waited for the EMTs to join him, and together they trudged toward the police truck.

"What's happened here, Carly? You didn't give me much information when you called," Paul asked.

"Sorry, Paul. I just needed you here in a hurry. We don't know what happened, but we found the two bodies about a half hour ago, buried in that drift over there at the end of the driveway. Scott and I came out here to check on things because we've been concerned about this family. Based on what we found, we should have checked a hell of a lot earlier. The animals are all dead in the barn. Starved to death from the looks of them," Carly said.

"Christ, I haven't come across anything like this up here since I started the job," Paul said. "All right, guys, let's take a look."

The six of them walked in a slow and silent procession to the roadside grave.

The group circled around the snow-covered bodies, trying to comprehend the enormity of the tragedy. Silk was still lying beside the body of the little girl, with his head on her chest. Carly called to him, but he refused to move. She finally grabbed his collar and pulled him away so that Paul Reynolds could get a closer look.

"The woman has obviously suffered some severe physical trauma or accident," Paul said. "But I'm not sure what has happened to the little girl. Where's Sean Malone? Any signs of him?"

"No sign of him anywhere, Paul," Carly replied.

"His truck is gone, maybe been gone for a few days now."

"Do you think he had anything to do with this?" Paul asked.

"I don't know, Paul, I truly don't," Carly replied. "But he is most definitely a person of interest right now. Problem is, we don't know where he is. Nobody's seen him since New Year's Day at the festival. Nobody's seen any of them. Emily Turner mentioned to Smitty a while back that she spoke with Sean right after the blizzard, but that's the only contact I know of that any one has had."

Scott helped the EMTs move the bodies down the snow-packed driveway and into the back of the ambulance. The flashing blue and red lights and the shrill sound of the sirens broke the morbid silence that had engulfed the tragic scene. Scott and Carly watched the small motorcade as it headed back toward town. Carly grabbed some yellow crime scene ribbons from the truck, and she and Scott marked off the property as best they could in the deep snow.

"We'd better start heading back, Scott," Carly said, "before it gets too stormy to see anything out here. We need to go right to the morgue so that we can fill out the reports for Paul."

They got into the truck and quieted Silk down before they started back toward town. Just before they left, Carly called the state trooper barracks in Burlington and had them put out an all-points bulletin to be on the lookout for Sean Malone and his white Ford pick-up truck. Scott hadn't driven a hundred yards when Carly started shivering violently again. He turned the heater up almost ten more degrees, but it didn't help, and her trembling continued for the entire ride to the county morgue.

It took them about a half hour to get to the coroner's building, and when they arrived, Paul was waiting in the front lobby for them. He took them to his office so that they could fill out the paperwork. When they finished, they thanked Paul and headed home. Scott dropped Carly off at her place.

"I'll stay with you tonight, Carly, if you want me to," he said.

"I think I am going to just grab something to eat and go to bed. Tomorrow's going to be a long day. Do you mind?"

It was obvious to Scott that Carly was evading him again about spending the night. This was the second time it had happened, and he wasn't quite sure why she continued to distance herself from him. "No, I'm tired myself, and I have some stuff to do at home," he said. "Call me if you need me, okay?"

"I will, Scott, but I'm hoping to get some sleep tonight. I'm exhausted."

He kissed her, hoping that she might change her mind, but she gently pushed him away.

"Go home! I'll see you in the morning," she said and turned to unlock her door. Carly didn't want him to know that she had other plans.

When she got in, she saw the message light blinking on her phone. There was a call from Rachel, asking how things were going. Carly dialed Rachel's number and was happy to hear her voice at the other end.

"Hi, Rach, just me returning your call."

"Carly, I'm so glad you called. I've had you on my mind all day. Just wondering how things were going," Rachel said.

"If you aren't sitting down, you'd better find a chair. This has been the second worst day in my entire life."

She spent the next fifteen minutes telling Rachel about what had happened, horrifying her with the gruesome details of what they had found.

"Carly, I don't know what to say. How awful! I'm so sorry. What happens now?"

"Scott and I have put an all-points bulletin out on Sean, and we'll start the search process right away. The troopers will be coming up from Burlington. We didn't find anything out there today that even gave us a clue as to his whereabouts. He could be anywhere for all we know right now."

Later that evening, she took Silk and headed back to Lakeview Farm alone. Even though she was officially off duty, she made sure that she had her handcuffs and service revolver on her belt. She had convinced herself that she was just going to look for numbers and addresses for Kate's family as well as Sean's, but she knew that her real motive was to try to find some clue, anything, that would help with the investigation. She knew Scott would be furious if he found out, but she thought she would do a better job of looking around if she was by herself. She figured she would take the heat from him later.

It had stopped snowing, but the night was devoid of light, with heavy dark clouds covering the full moon. The air was frigid, causing an icy crust to form on the new snowfall. When Carly arrived at Lakeview Farm, she had to use her largest flashlight to illuminate the Malones' driveway. She picked her way carefully along the tire tracks that they had made earlier, trying to avoid a slip on the icy surface. Silk had difficulty moving in the frozen snow and sunk to his chest with each footstep he took. Carly was totally focused on making her way to the back door of the house, and she didn't notice that the garage door was open or that there were tire tracks across the yard and in front of the garage.

The back door leading to the kitchen was open. Carly distinctly remembered locking it when they left earlier in the day, at least she thought she had locked it. She entered the kitchen with caution, trying not to make a sound as she moved about. The house was darker than the night, and she put her flashlight on its highest beam to light her way in the room. Silk was at her side, and she told him to be quiet as she moved forward in the room. There was no evidence that the heat or any electrical appliances were on anywhere. Carly's attention was suddenly drawn to a strange clicking sound coming from the counter, near the sink. Moving the beam of her flashlight toward the noise, she saw two small dark shadows moving back and forth across the countertop. Crows again. They had managed to get into the empty house through the open back door. Their beady yellow eyes followed her as she came toward them, and their long talons clicked on the hard granite as their bodies moved back and forth along the polished stone. Silk saw them and broke free from his leash, snapping and growling at the black birds. He lunged, nearly catching one of them, but they escaped, squawking angrily as they flew through the open kitchen door.

Carly was frightened by the surprise encounter, and it took her a minute to compose herself. She closed the kitchen door and moved her flashlight beam around the room again until it landed on a small writing desk in the corner. She rummaged through the drawers until she found an old address book, and holding the light to the pages, she saw names and phone numbers for Kate's parents and sister. There was a number for what she thought might be Sean's sister as well. Placing the address book in her jacket pocket, she left the kitchen and moved quietly into the family room, stopping suddenly at the bottom of the staircase. Someone else was in the house. She could feel it, a presence in the room with her, and her imagination began to run away with her reason. She could almost feel warm breath on the back of her neck. She tried to tell herself it was just her imagination running wild, but fear nearly paralyzed her, and her breathing became shallow and rapid. "Stop it. Stop it," she whispered to herself. "Get a grip and keep moving."

She didn't turn around but, instead, reached for her holster, opening the safety buckle on her belt, and slowly removed her revolver. Silk stood close to her with his hackles raised along the full length of his back, growling in a low rumble from deep in his throat. There was a large framed mirror directly in front of Carly, and her flashlight threw enough beam to let her see her reflection and that of the room behind her. She stared into the glass, trying to detect any movement in the room.

Something, a shadow, a flicker of motion, caught her attention as it floated along the wall at the far end of the family room. Then it disappeared as quickly as it came. Still facing the mirror, Carly eased her flashlight down quietly until it touched the stairs. She made sure that the beam projected across the room behind her. She brought her revolver to her side and raised it as quietly as she could. Grabbing Silk by the collar with her free hand, she turned slowly to face the other end of the room. Whatever she thought she saw a moment ago was gone, but the feeling that she was not alone remained.

There were only two exits from the family room, the kitchen entrance and the staircase. She picked up her flashlight and released Silk from his lead. He dashed forward into the kitchen, barking ferociously. Carly followed him, one hand holding her flashlight and the other clasped around the gun, which she was now holding at arm's length in front of her, ready to fire. There was a commotion in the kitchen, followed by the crashing sound of overturned furniture. Silk was snarling, and she could hear the scraping sounds of his paws as he tried to get traction on the tile floor. As soon as she got through the kitchen door, she saw the dog growling and snapping at a figure on the floor. He had it pinned beneath the overturned kitchen table, and when she flashed her light under the table, she saw Sean Malone's terrified look as he tried to protect his face from the attacking animal.

He looked at Carly, pleading. "Get him off me, Carly. Get him off me! He's trying to get at my throat!"

She held the light on them and aimed the gun at Sean's chest.

"Silk, no! Back off!" she called to the dog.

He moved away from Sean, still growling, teeth bared.

"Sean, get up on your knees and put your hands behind your head. Now!"

She pushed the table aside with her leg and moved closer to Sean, still aiming her gun at him.

His neck and arm were bleeding from the dog's bites, but he obeyed Carly and got to his knees, locking his hands and arms behind his head.

Carly put the flashlight on the counter, focusing its light on Sean while she dialed Scott on her cell phone. Silk stood in front of Sean in an attack-ready position, waiting for a command from Carly.

It was late, and Scott was just about ready to go to bed when his phone rang.

"Scott, it's Carly. I need you at the Malone house right now. I have Sean Malone here and need the cruiser."

"Carly, what—" he started to ask.

"Scott, don't ask me anything right now. Just get here as fast as you can."

"Okay, okay. On my way," he said. "But you have some explaining to do!"

She ended the call, and with her gun still aimed at Sean, she repositioned him. "I want you to lie down on your stomach, Sean, and put your hands behind your back."

He complied without a word, and she handcuffed him then stepped quickly away from him.

"Sean Malone," she said, "I'm taking you into custody. You are a prime suspect in the murder of Kate and Maura Malone. Don't even think of moving and don't say a word, or I swear to God, I'll put this dog on you again, and this time I won't call him off!"

Sean remained silent with his head on the floor, and his face turned away from Carly. She watched anxiously for Scott to show up, checking the kitchen window for signs of the flashing blue lights.

Scott arrived about ten minutes later, flooding the yard with light from the police cruiser. He had a portable utility light with him and turned it on when he entered the kitchen door. Without saying a word to Carly, he grabbed Sean by the jacket and lifted him to a standing position. Carly moved to help him, but he pushed her away. "I've got him. Just open the back door of the cruiser so I can get him in there."

Carly walked out of the kitchen ahead of Scott and made her way down the icy driveway. Silk stayed at her side, turning every few steps to look at Scott. Scott followed close behind with Sean, holding his hand on Sean's head as he eased him into the back seat of the vehicle. When he turned to face the house again, he noticed the open garage door, and Sean's white truck sitting beside Kate's SUV. But his attention went back to Carly as soon as he locked Sean into his seat and closed the door.

He glared at her. "Okay, hotshot," Scott said. "What are you doing out here by yourself? Are you crazy? You just can't leave things along, can you? You could've been killed out here! Why didn't you let me know you were doing this? I would've come with you. You know that! I can't believe you did this!"

He was furious with her, and she decided to keep her mouth shut and take the heat rather than fuel the fire more. He waited for a response, and getting none, he got into the cruiser, still shaking his head in disbelief. Carly waited until he left the driveway before getting into her own car and heading back. She followed Scott back to town, parking behind him when they got to the station. Together they escorted Sean into the police station, booked him, got his fingerprints, and then seated him, still in handcuffs, in the conference room near the front entrance. Scott took Carly to the outside office once Sean was settled.

"Would you kindly tell me what the hell you think you were doing out there by yourself tonight?"

"I'll tell you everything later. Please let's just interrogate this guy and see if we can get a confession out of him," she said. "I'll do up the arrest report, and you take over as the investigating officer because we need to recommend to the DA's office that criminal charges should be filed with a probable cause statement by morning. We can't detain him for very long without the prosecutor actually filing charges!"

Scott agreed.

"Did you read him his Miranda yet?

"Not yet. I'll do it when we go back in there with him."

Sean watched them, trying to pick up what they are saying, but their voices were too quiet for him to hear any of the conversation clearly. Scott and Carly walked back into the conference room together, each one taking a seat on either side of Sean. Carly started by handing him a copy of his Miranda and reading it to him at the same time.

"Sean Malone, you are under arrest for the murder of your wife, Kathleen Malone, and your daughter, Maura Malone. You have the right to remain silent. Anything you say can and will be held against you in a court of law. You have the right to an attorney. If you can't afford an attorney, the court will appoint one for you. Do you understand your rights?" Sean looked up at her with a belligerent stare.

"I understand."

"Do you have an attorney, or do you want the court to appoint an attorney?" Carly asked.

"No, and I have no money to pay for one. You'll have to arrange for a court-appointed attorney for me," he told her.

Carly got up again.

"I'm going to the front desk to write up the police report for the DA, Scott. Be right back."

She headed out to the front office and pulled up the online form to fill it out and submit it to the district attorney's office electronically. At the same time, she pulled up the template that would let her create a confession form to be signed in the event that Sean actually did confess. They planned to interrogate him as much as they could without a lawyer present. How much they could get away with remained to be seen. If Sean was willing to talk, they could question him about anything. They could even lie to him if it got them closer to getting his signed confession. Just before she finished the printouts, she sent an electronic request to the Vermont State Police, requesting a complete background check on Sean Malone. They knew very little about him, and Carly decided it was time that they learned. The background check reports would be back to them by morning, along with some reply from the prosecutor.

Carly printed out both documents and brought them back into the conference room with her. She took the confession form and slid it across the table so that it landed in front of Sean.

"You'd better read that, Sean. We're going to be looking for a signature from you," Carly said.

Sean stared down at the confession form. "I'm not signing this," he said, pushing the document back across the table to Carly.

"Sean, did you kill your wife and daughter?" Scott asked him. "And you'd better tell me straight because we have pretty good evidence to say that you did."

"No, I did *not* kill them," he answered.

"Then what were you doing skulking around the house tonight? You knew we would find those bodies."

No answer.

"What happened to the animals, Sean?" Carly asked. "We found all of them dead. Frozen to the ground in their stalls. Did you just let them starve to death?"

"I didn't have any money for feed, so I left town to find work," Sean replied. "Kate and Maura were fine when I left. So were the animals. I thought Kate would take care of them."

"You knew she couldn't take care of them, Sean. There was no feed in the barn for any of them," Carly said.

"When did you leave Lakeview Farm?" Scott asked him.

"About a week ago," Sean replied.

"Did you find work?"

"No, that's why I came back tonight."

"So what happened to Kate and Maura, Sean? They didn't get into that snowbank all by themselves," Carly questioned.

"I don't know. I told you. I just got back tonight," Sean replied.

"You don't seem very upset that your wife and little girl were found dead, Sean," Scott said. "Why is that? I would think you would be overwhelmed with grief right about now. Wouldn't you think that, Officer Richardson?"

Scott looked directly at Carly, wanting her to pick up the volley.

"Yeah, why is that, Sean? I'm confused. Why don't you tell us why you're not upset that your family has been murdered?"

Carly was standing and staring directly down at Sean.

He stared back at her, smirking. "I'm not saying anything until I have a lawyer here," Sean told them. He sat back in his seat, staring straight ahead at the wall in front of him.

"Okay, Sean. Have it your way, but I'm going back out to that house tonight, and I'm going to bring back some indisputable evidence that you *do* know what happened. Why don't you just tell us and save me the trip?" Scott said.

Sean continued to stare in silence at the blank wall.

"I'm just trying to make this a little easier on you, but we can play this out any way you want, Sean," Scott told him.

Carly walked over to Sean and grabbed him under both arms from behind, helping him to a standing position.

"C'mon with me, Sean," she said. "You're going to be our guest for a night or two."

Scott opened the conference room door for them.

"I'll take him from here, Carly," he said. "Will you call Bill Salter down in Burlington and see if he can get up here tomorrow and represent Mr. Malone?"

Carly waited until Scott had led Sean into the cellblock area before she went back out to the office to call the lawyer.

Scott moved Sean ahead of him and got him through the door to the holding cell area. The two cells were small, about ten by ten, with a cot, a sink and toilet, and a small desk and chair in each one. Woolen blankets, some sheets, and a pillow were at the foot of each cot. The floors were bare concrete, and the single window was set high and protected with vertical iron bars. The cell doors were electrically locked and unlocked with a switch at the entrance to the cellblock area. They were seldom used, so they were in a clean and well-maintained condition.

Scott directed Sean into the first cell, closing the cell door once he was inside.

"Sean, I'm going to ask you to back up against the cell bars so I can remove your handcuffs. After I do, I want you to remove all your clothing, except underwear, and put on the orange jumpsuit at the foot of the cot. There are some slippers there, too. Put your clothes, shoes, wallet, watch, and anything else on your person into the box at the foot of the bed, then hand me the box so it can be locked in the evidence room. Do you understand?" Scott ordered.

"Yeah, I understand," Sean answered sullenly.

Scott unlocked the handcuffs and stood back, hand on his revolver, while Sean undressed and got himself into the prison issue suit. He placed all his personal items in the box and then proceeded to hand Scott the box as instructed.

Scott tested the cell door to be sure the lock was fast and then left the cellblock without saying anything further to Sean Malone.

Sean sat on the hard cot mattress, staring at the wall in front of him. He looked up at the small barred window then put his head in his hands and cried silently in the dark cell.

THIRTY-FIVE

Carly was on the phone when Scott returned to the front office. She motioned for him to be quiet while she left a message for the attorney. When she finished, she hung up, looking sheepishly at Scott who was hovering over her, scowling.

"Well? Are you going to tell me what you were doing at Lakeview Farm—alone, at night?" he asked.

"I know, I know. It was stupid, but I just had a feeling that Sean was either there, or he left some clue as to where he might be. I just knew it, and I thought if I waited until morning, the opportunity to get him would be gone."

"Okay, so why didn't you call me to go out there with you? You knew when I left you that you were going to go there tonight, didn't you?"

His frustration with her was written all over his face.

"What was so important about going out there by yourself, Carly? What if he had been armed? What if he had come after you? You could've been killed out there."

"Scott, it was just something I had to do. I couldn't tell you. You would have stopped me. I know you don't understand, and yes, I know it was probably stupid, but she was my friend, Scott. And I know he killed her. I didn't want to take the chance that he would get away or get too far away. You would've talked me out of going, I know you would have. And we got him, didn't we? And I'm okay. Nothing happened."

"Picking at the threads again, Carly. Always picking at the threads! Just can't leave things alone, can you?"

"I know, but this time, it's a good thing that I didn't leave things alone, isn't it?"

Scott wanted to stay angry, but he couldn't do it. "Carly, you are impossible. You worry me sometimes," he said as he started to walk away. But then he stopped, his back still to her, and turned around. "If I didn't love you, then I guess it wouldn't matter, would it? I could have lost you out there tonight. Now go on home with Silk. I'll stay here for tonight and keep an eye on our guest."

"Okay, Scott. I'll be here early in the morning. And…thank you. For everything," she said. "Do you want me to leave Silk here with you for the night?" she asked.

"No, you take him home. I think you could use the company," Scott replied. "I'm going back out to that house because I want to check to see if I can turn up anything interesting," he said. "Sean will be all right until I get back. I'll make sure he has some dinner before I leave."

He walked out to the car with her and stood watching as she pulled away from her parking space and into the street. She turned and waved to him before she drove away. It was still snowing, and her windshield wipers were working hard at keeping the accumulation to a minimum as she drove.

She collapsed on the sofa the minute she got home. The events of the day were numbing, and she couldn't clear her mind of the image of Kate and Maura lying in an icy hole. The phone rang, and she thought about not answering it but noticed on the caller ID that it was coming from her father's cell phone. This was a surprise call, and she hesitated a moment before picking up.

"Hello, Dad."

"Carly, Rachel told me what happened. Are you all right?"

"I've had better days, but yes, I'm all right."

"Do you want me to come up there? Because if you do, I'll get in the car right now."

"No, please, Dad. Not necessary. But I appreciate the offer, and I promise I will let you know if I need you here."

"Do you feel like talking about it now?"

"Not right now. I just want to get to bed. Maybe tomorrow. And, Dad, thank you for calling. You have no idea how much I appreciate it."

George's call took her completely by surprise, and she wasn't sure if she should be happy or angry with Rachel for letting him know what had happened. She thought about calling Rachel, but instead, she took a hot shower and got into bed, falling asleep before the ten o'clock news. She had slipped easily into a dream-free sleep when she was awakened by the ring of the phone.

"Carly? It's Scott. Hey, I found something out at the farm. I'm coming to your place. You need to see this."

She started to ask him what was so urgent, but he hung up before she could say anything. She got up and put on her robe and slippers and went into the kitchen to make some hot chocolate. Silk was whining at the door, and she let him out while she put some cups on the kitchen table. Within ten minutes, Scott was pounding at the front door.

He pushed past her, holding a plastic bag with something in it in his hand.

"Look at this," he said. "Tell me what you think this is."

Carly took the bag from him, careful not to touch the contents. It looked like some fragments of cloth with blood stains on them.

"Where did you find these, Scott?" she asked. "It looks like blood-stained fabric. Wool maybe."

"I found these pieces stuck to the edge of the plow on Sean's truck. I am pretty sure these are pieces of fabric from Kate's winter coat. Can't be sure until I check with the coroner's office, but I'd be willing to bet on it. If it is, Carly, this is the evidence we need to get the prosecutor to file criminal charges!"

"We need to be careful with this, Scott. Can't contaminate it. Did you have gloves on when you removed the pieces?"

"Absolutely. This is the break we need to link Sean to those murders, Carly. I wasn't going to take a chance on damaging it."

She knew he was right. "Kate's coat was brown, just like this material."

"This is almost unimaginable, but do you think he ran Kate down with that plow?" she asked.

"Wouldn't surprise me one bit. I think anyone who left animals in the condition that this bastard did is capable of anything, Carly."

"But why? Why would he do something that terrible? And what about Maura? Oh my God. Did he run her down, too?"

Carly sat down in one of the kitchen chairs, looking at the pieces of blood-stained wool on the kitchen table.

It was almost one o'clock in the morning when they decided that they would go back to the police station and haul Sean back into the conference room for further interrogation. They unlocked the heavy door to the cellblock and turned on the bright fluorescent lights. Sean was curled up on the cot in a fetal position with the wool blanket pulled over his head. Scott took his nightstick from his belt.

"Watch this. I'll give him a little wake up call," he said.

He ran the metal stick along the cell bars, making a horrendous racket and scaring Sean straight off the cot and onto the floor.

"Hey, Sean! Top o' the mornin' to ya," Scott yelled. "We thought we'd get an early start today. Just got a few more questions to ask you, so come on, get up, and put your back to the bars with your arms behind you so I can put the cuffs on you."

Sean, still half-asleep, stumbled across the cell floor and put his back to the bar as he was told. Scott cuffed him and directed Sean to the cell door.

"C'mon now, Sean. We're going to have another little chat," Scott said.

Carly opened the cell door, and Scott reached in and directed Sean through the heavy metal door. He moved him into the front office and, grabbing him by the elbow, led him into the conference room again.

"C'mon, man. Gimme a break. What time is it? It's still dark out," Sean said.

"Never mind the time," Scott told him. I want you to take a very close look at something."

He placed the plastic bag in front of Sean.

"Recognize this?" Scott asked him.

Sean looked at the pieces of fabric for a moment, showing no expression on his face at all.

"Nope. Never saw it before. What is it?" he asked.

"Look again, Sean," Carly told him. "Where do you think we found this stuff?"

"I have no bloody idea. Where did you find it?"

"On the edge of your truck's snowplow. Just stuck there, probably from the blood that's on it. This is fabric from Kate's coat, Sean! How did it get blood on it and stuck to your plow? It didn't just get there by accident, Sean!" Carly was yelling at him, hoping that he would break down.

"You ran that plow into her Sean, didn't you? You killed your wife and baby girl with your plow, didn't you? We know you did it, Sean, so why don't you just admit it and make it easier on yourself."

Changing her tack, she softened her voice a little, hoping to get a reaction from him.

"C'mon, Sean. Make it easy on yourself. Why don't you tell us what happened out there?"

For just an instant, Carly thought he might open up. He looked worn out, and there was the slightest change in his demeanor that made her think she might get a response from him. But the moment passed, and Sean pulled himself together.

"I told you before, I want a lawyer. I'm not answering any more of your questions without a lawyer, so you can just take me back to my cell. You're wasting your time and mine," he said.

"Okay. We'll play it your way, Sean. But don't look for any favors from us," Carly said.

She brought him back to his cell while Scott stayed behind her and held the heavy door for them.

"That was a huge waste of time," she said to Scott as they walked back to the main office. "I thought for sure we'd get something out of him, didn't you?"

"Yeah, for a minute I did, but he just clammed up. It's interesting that he won't look at you directly, isn't it? You've been talking about that right along, but I never noticed it before tonight. What is that all about, I wonder?"

"I have no idea," Carly replied. "But he certainly avoids eye contact with me. And, you know, I *still* have that feeling that I know him from someplace. Which reminds me, I notified the state guys to do a background check on him. We don't know a thing about this guy other than the few things Kate mentioned. For all we know, he might have a rap sheet a mile long!"

"Let's hope we get some of the information back in the morning. Why don't you go home and try to get a little sleep, Carly," Scott told her. "Silk's alone back there, too. I'll be fine here. Just try to get back around eight in the morning, okay?"

Carly wanted to kiss him right then but instead gave him a quick hug and a pat on the cheek.

"I'll see you in a couple of hours," she said, thinking that this was neither the right time nor place for anything romantic.

THIRTY-SIX

Attorney William Salter arrived at the Saint Basile Police Department door at precisely 8:30 a.m. dressed like a disheveled Vermont game warden in a thread-bare field jacket and fur-lined cap. He was carrying a beaten-up brown leather briefcase that looked as if it would burst its seams at the slightest bump. The cap was pulled down over his ears so that only a small part of his face was showing. Carly had arrived only minutes before and was just pouring herself a mug of hot coffee when Scott let him in. She had to hide her surprise at his appearance by keeping herself busy with the coffeepot. His looks proved to be deceiving because he was all about business, and after brief introductions, the lawyer was ready to get to work.

"I would like to see my client right away if possible," he said.

"I presume that you have not questioned him or forced any type of confession from him?"

"We have questioned him but didn't get much out of him," Scott answered. We read him his rights, and he acknowledged understanding them. The state police were notified, and we requested a background check that we hope to see in the next hour or so."

"Mr. Salter, we would like to be present while you are questioning your client," Carly said.

"I'm afraid that I can't permit that, officer. I need to speak with him privately first. I'll call you in if I think there is a need to have you in there," the lawyer replied. "Have you received any reports back at all from the medical examiner?" he asked.

"Not yet. We are expecting those this morning as well. We're still not quite sure how the victims died, and we're anxious to see the coroner's report," Scott replied. "We haven't been able to reach the families of the victims either. Officer Richardson has tried contacting them but has not connected yet. If we don't reach them today, we'll put the state police on it. We're pretty sure that the family members are still in Massachusetts. Why don't you go into the conference room, Mr. Salter, and I'll bring the prisoner in to you. Just give me a couple of minutes to get him ready. Carly, show Mr. Salter in, would you please?"

Carly showed the lawyer into the conference room while Scott went into the cellblock to get Sean. She waited until he was seated and settled with his paperwork before she headed out to the front office to check the fax. They were waiting for the reports from the medical examiner and the background check from the Vermont State Police. There were several sheets of paper in the fax machine, and Carly could see from the cover sheet that they had come in from the coroner's office. These were the autopsy reports they had requested.

They revealed some shocking detail. Kate had suffered a broken leg and a broken arm, and the cause of her death had been a blow to the back of her head with a large blunt object. Maura did not have any broken bones, but there were bruises on her arms and legs, and the cause of death appeared to be suffocation. The medical examiner was convinced that Maura's suffocation was the result of the weight of something heavy on her chest. His report suggested that the child was still alive when she was buried in the snowdrift.

Scott was just leaving the conference room when she motioned him to join her at the front desk.

"Look at this! Just came in from Paul's office. Confirms what we suspected, Scott. Kate was hit by the blade of the plow on Sean's truck. It's not quite as clear what happened to Maura, but it appears that she suffocated."

"Let me see them, Carly," Scott said. She handed the six-page report to him and watched his reaction as he read it. She could tell from his expression that he was disgusted by the coroner's report.

Scott paced back and forth, fuming as he moved. "He just mowed the two of them down with his plow! So help me, God, I would like to go in there and wring his bloody murdering neck."

"Scott, calm down. We have no confession. Don't forget that! But I do think we have a pretty solid case against him. Let's just wait until we hear back from the DA's office. It's still early," Carly said.

"Yeah, you're right. You've been right about this guy all along. I could kick myself for not listening to you and stepping in earlier to help Kate."

"Don't go beating yourself up over it now. You were right, too, you know. We didn't have anything substantial to go on then. I was the one pushing, and you, rightfully, kept the lid on things. I don't know if this could have been prevented, I really don't. At least, I don't know if *we* could have prevented it."

The fax line rang again, and they both turned to see another report coming through, this time from the state police.

"That must be the background check," Scott said as he walked over to get the papers.

"Wonder what the staties have turned up on this guy!"

Scott grabbed the papers from the machine and brought them to Carly.

Two disturbing bits of information about Sean Malone surfaced from the background check. There was a report of a prior court issue almost two years back that detailed a vehicular homicide event near Cambridge. It involved an accident on December 27, 2009, at which time a Robert Emmet Shaw was killed by the plow blade on the truck driven by Michael Sean Malone, aka Sean Malone.

Carly's face drained of color, and she read no further. Scott looked at her, waiting for her to say something. She read the documents a second time and then handed the papers to Scott. Her name was mentioned as a witness to the accident. No indictment was made as the event was deemed "an accident caused by extraordinary weather."

"Carly…" Scott started to say something to her.

"Don't, Scott. Please. Don't say anything."

Still holding the report, she walked over to the leather chair in front of the reception desk and sank down into the soft cushioned seat.

"I was right, Scott. I was right all along," she said. "I did know him. I could feel it all along. It wasn't just déjà vu. It was real. He killed Rob, Scott. It was him. He knew me right from the beginning! Right from the first time I saw him! That's why he wouldn't look at me! That's why he didn't want me around Kate. This explains everything! He's not going to get away with this again, Scott. He's not. Not while I have a breath left in my body, he's not. I'll see him dead before he gets away with this again."

She was in a rage. Scott had never seen her like this, and she was scaring him. She grabbed the report from his hand and headed for the conference room.

"Carly, don't!" Scott yelled at her. "Don't go in there with them! Please!"

She turned and gave him an icy look, and without answering, she burst into the conference room and flung the papers in front of Sean.

"You knew all along, you murderer, didn't you? You knew who I was. You knew, and you never said a word to me. You never told Kate either, did you? Let me tell you something, Michael Sean Malone, you won't get away with this. Rob might have been an accident, but Kate and Maura, they were not an accident, and I'm going to see you pay for it. If I have to kill you myself, you're going to pay for it."

Bill Salter jumped up from his seat.

"Officer Richardson, I must ask you to leave immediately. This is highly inappropriate, and you are on the fringe of violating Mr. Malone's legal rights here," he said. "I insist that you refrain from saying anything further to my client."

"Legal rights? Legal rights? As far as I'm concerned, this murderer has no rights," Carly screamed at the lawyer. She tried to move around him to get at Sean when Scott came into the room.

"Carly, stop!" he boomed. "Stop right now. Don't say one more thing. Sorry for the disturbance, Mr. Salter. We won't bother you again. Officer Richardson, please, leave counsel with his client and come with me."

Scott took Carly by the arm and led her out of the conference room. Sean folded his arms and put his head down on them, his face on the table. The lawyer closed the door and took his seat across the table from him again, not quite sure what to say about the sudden intrusion.

"You came very close to getting yourself in real trouble in there, Carly. What was that all about? You could have ruined this case for us on a technicality. You should know better than to interfere with due process like that. I don't care how upset you are about this. That was just plain wrong, Carly! Wrong!"

He stood waiting for her to say something.

"Okay. Okay. Sorry. I just saw red when I looked at that report. This guy—he's a killer, Scott. He's a walking time bomb, and he'll do it again if he gets the chance. He didn't *murder* Rob. I know that. But he didn't get anything more than a slap on the wrist either. But he did murder his wife and daughter, and I'm going to make sure that he gets more than a slap on the wrist this time."

"Carly, you have to let the process do the work. You have to stay out of this. Salter could get this whole thing dismissed when we get before the judge."

He managed to quiet her down but was worried that she might go off and do some damage when he wasn't around.

"Carly, promise me that you won't interfere with this," Scott said.

"Okay, okay, I promise. But they can't get him into the courtroom soon enough as far as I'm concerned," she said.

THIRTY-SEVEN

The attorney finished up with Sean around noon time. He called for either Scott or Carly to take Sean back to the cellblock.

"I'll take him, Carly. Just get Salter out of here," Scott said.

Scott led Sean out of the conference room and back to the cellblock while Carly got the attorney's coat and hat from the closet.

"Officer Richardson, that was an unnecessary scene you pulled in there a while ago," he said, taking his coat from her. "You're lucky I didn't insist on getting him dismissed out of here. I've talked to the DA, and bail has been set at $100,000 for Mr. Malone. Since we don't see any chance of him paying that, he will be here until the arraignment, which is day after tomorrow. I trust you can treat him in a professional manner until then," he said.

"I assure you, Mr. Salter, there will be no repeats. We'll see you in court," Carly replied curtly.

She showed him out and went back toward the cellblock to find Scott. Silk was whining at the door to go out, and instead of going into the cellblock, she grabbed his collar and leash from the coat hook.

"C'mon, boy. I can use a walk myself."

She got on the intercom to get Scott's attention.

"Hey," she said. "I'm going to take Silk for a walk. Be back in a few minutes, okay?"

The dark skies were pregnant with snow-filled clouds. There were a few people walking along the sidewalk, and several children passed, towing their Christmas sleds and ice skates as they headed toward the town common. Silk was tugging at the leash, anxious to run and play with them, but Carly pulled him back, asking him to heel as she walked past the police department building. Her cell phone rang just as she started to head downtown. It was Rachel. Carly had been so involved with Sean Malone's capture that she hadn't remembered to call Rachel and bring her up-to-date.

"Hi, Rach, sorry I didn't call you earlier," Carly said.

"That's okay. I just called to wish you Happy New Year," Rachel replied.

"My dad called me. I wasn't sure whether to thank you or be mad at you for contacting him, but I was happy to hear from him."

"I had to call him, Carly. I was so worried about you after you told me what had happened to that family. I thought he might be able to help."

It's okay, Rachel. I'm glad that you told him."

"So what's going on now?" Rachel asked.

"We arrested Sean Malone yesterday for the murder of Kate and Maura."

She could hear Rachel let out a gasp at the other end.

"That's not all," she continued. "You won't believe this, but a background check came back and identified him as the same person who was driving the truck the night Rob was killed. He killed Rob, Rachel. Just plowed into him and then did the same thing to his wife and child!"

"Are you sure, Carly? How do you know for sure?" Rachel asked.

"Because his ID picture was the same, and the police report named me as a witness to that accident. He changed his name when he came up here. His real name is Michael Sean Malone. I never knew his full name because I didn't want to know it. My dad handled all that paperwork for me and never brought it up. He knew it was me all the time, Rachel. He knew, and he never said a word to me or Kate. That's why I had that odd feeling about him, you know, like I had met him before or something. Remember, I kept telling you I thought I knew him from someplace?"

"Oh my God, Carly. What's going to happen now?" Rachel asked.

"Well, he's locked up with us right now, and we expect the arraignment to happen the day after tomorrow. I almost lost it with him today when I saw that report from the state troopers. Scott is furious with me because he said I could have blown the case. So I have to stay away from Sean Malone for now."

"I suppose I know the answer to this already, but by any chance, have you called your father about what you did?" Rachel asked.

"No, I haven't, but I suppose I should," Carly replied. "I might need a lawyer myself before this is over."

"Carly, I'm going to call him now, okay? I'll just fill him in and tell him you may need his help. Would that be all right?"

"That would be a huge help, Rachel. I just don't feel like talking to him about all of this right now. Thanks. Listen, I have to go. Silk is anxious to get walking and…oh no…it's snowing *again*!"

Carly hung up and started to walk at a brisk pace with Silk. He trotted along beside her, waving his feathered tail back and forth like a flag as he moved. He spotted a group of children up ahead and pulled at the leash, trying to get Carly to move faster so he could join in their fun. When they got to the town commons, Carly let him off the leash, and he ran toward a group of children who were skating on the frozen frog pond. They all knew him and called him to join them on the ice. Carly couldn't help smiling as she watched him slipping along on the ice as he tried to keep up with the skaters. It was snowing hard by then, but she stayed for a little while longer before calling Silk back to her. There was already an accumulation of over an inch, and from the looks of the sky, she expected there would be several more inches before the day was done. She was on duty that night, and she wanted to get back to the department building before the weather got much worse.

By dusk, the snow had accumulated another five inches. The plows were out and were keeping the streets just barely passable. Most of the smaller merchants had closed down for the day and were making their way home, emptying the streets and sidewalks of traffic. Carly turned the office radio on when she got back. Scott was busy bringing some dinner to Sean, and she sat at his desk listening to the weather station. The forecast predicted the storm to last overnight with a total accumulation of over twenty-five inches. The wind had already picked up, and she could see from where she was sitting that it was blowing snow into high drifts in some places along the street. It howled around the corners of the building, sending snow in swirls around the columns at the front entrance. Scott came back after a few minutes with Sean's dinner plates. The food had hardly been touched. "Not eating, huh?" she said. "He ought to be left to starve the same way his animals were left."

Scott didn't say anything back. He just brought the dishes into the kitchenette, and she could hear him scraping them off into the rubbish and then washing them in the sink.

She got up and went in to the kitchenette with him.

"Sorry about today. What I did was pretty dumb. I just lost it," she said.

"I know. But look, there's nothing more you or I can do right now, so just try to make the best of it until this case gets in front of the judge, okay?"

"Okay," she replied.

"Scott, I'll stay here tonight with Silk and keep the watch. It's my turn to be on overnight call anyway."

She could see Scott's shoulders tense as he continued what he was doing at the sink.

"Do you think that's smart, Carly? I'm not sure I like that idea at all. I'm not sure you'll mind your business and stay away from him!" Scott finally said. "Why don't you let me stay, and you go on home."

"No, Scott. It's my night on call. I'll stay. I won't go near him, I promise. You've done enough, and you look exhausted. *You* go home and get a good night's sleep. I'll call you if I need you."

"Okay, Carly. Guess I won't change your mind on this one." His tone of voice sounded aggravated to her.

"Are you angry with me?" she asked him.

"No, not angry. You just puzzle me sometimes. I never know what to expect with you. Maybe I should just learn to expect the unexpected, then there would be no surprises."

She walked up to him and took his face in her hands, kissing him lightly on each side of his face.

"In case you didn't know, Scott Eames, I think I may have fallen in love with you too. So there. Now I've said it to you. That must make us even, don't you think?"

Just as abruptly, she turned from him and went back to the main room.

"And I am staying here tonight. No argument," she said.

Scott closed up the small kitchen area and went back to the main room as well. He grabbed his coat from the rack and sat to pull on his high boots.

"Your truck is buried half up the wheels, Scott. Want me to help you dig out?" Carly asked.

"No, I'm okay. I'll get it. You make sure that you lock up behind me. There's extra wood in the closet for the stove. Make sure you have the fire up high enough. It's going to get frigid tonight. Are you sure you'll be okay?"

"Yes, for God's sake. I have Silk with me. Go home. I'll call you if I need you."

She reached up and playfully tugged his hat down over his eyes.

"Now get out of here!" she said, pushing him toward the door.

She locked up behind Scott and went to check the dead bolts on the cellblock door to make sure they were locked. She made sure that the overhead light in the corridor of the block was still on and then walked back to the woodstove, stoking the glowing embers and adding some fresh wood to keep the room temperature steady.

The thermostat read sixty-eight, but she was suddenly chilled to the bone. She grabbed the heavy wool sweater from the back of her desk chair and put a quilted vest on over it. Scott had left some chili heating on top of the stove for her, and she grabbed a bowl and spoon from the kitchenette, remembering that she hadn't eaten anything since breakfast. There was dog food in the refrigerator, and she fixed a plate for Silk as well. When they both had finished eating, they sat side by side in front of the cast-iron stove, warmed by the burning coals in the stove's belly. The quiet was shattered by the ring of her cell phone. Her father was on the line.

"Hi, Dad. Rachel must have called you," she said.

"She told me what happened with the lawyer today. Did you manage to get things under control?"

"I think so, but I was going to call you because I may need some legal help if Mr. Salter decides to press the issue."

She went on to explain her unfortunate outburst in front of Sean's attorney, half expecting to be reprimanded for it. Instead, George just listened, which was totally out of character for him. When she finished telling him what had happened, she asked what he thought about the situation.

"Well, you may have jeopardized your case against this guy, Carly, but I'm more concerned about the threat that you made. That might be a serious issue. My suggestion…let's just wait until the arraignment in a few days. I think you'll know which way the wind is blowing once that happens. Do you want me to drive up there and attend the court session?"

"No, Dad. I'll be okay. I'll let you know if you need to come up."

"Carly, one more thing. I'm so sorry for the way I've acted with you. I am so very sorry. I hope you'll forgive me. What I said to you was just plain wrong, and I guess I was too much of an egomaniac to apologize sooner. I'm glad you're okay, honey. I love you. You know I do. I'm just not very good at saying it I guess."

Carly was surprised by the apology. It was the first time in her entire life that she had ever heard him apologize for anything. She could barely answer him.

"Dad…I don't know what to say. I love you too. And thank you," she finally replied.

By seven o'clock, the snow was falling in huge wet clumps, sticking to everything it touched. Carly looked out the front door thinking that almost a foot had accumulated since the afternoon, increasing by at least an inch an hour. The tree branches, already stressed by the wet loads accumulating on them, started snapping off from the weight. Main Street was empty and silent except for the constant cracking sound of breaking branches. Carly turned on the TV in the main office to get the evening news. Storm warnings and dire reports were breaking on every local channel. One forecaster predicted that there will be over three feet accumulating by noon the following day, with no letup in sight until evening.

She checked the monitor to keep a watch on Sean. He had fallen asleep on the small bunk bed with the coarse woolen jail blanket tossed over him. The cellblock had electric heat and stayed comfortably warm most of the time. That section of the building was a fairly new addition and well insulated. The main part of the building was old and drafty, with very little insulation in many areas. The woodstove was cranked and kept the rooms generally warm. Carly added a few more logs, hoping they would carry through until morning. She checked on Sean a final time at around ten thirty and found him still asleep in the same position he was in earlier in the evening. She was tired and stretched out on the office sofa, wrapping herself in a threadbare patchwork quilt. Even with the woodstove running hot and Carly clothed in a heavy sweater and a vest, she couldn't get rid of that gnawing, bone-deep chill she had been feeling all day. She fell asleep shivering, with Silk curled up at her feet.

Around five o'clock, Carly was awakened from a deep sleep by a loud crash outside the front windows. Silk leapt from the couch, barking. She jumped up tangled in the old quilt to see what has caused the noise. The wood fire had died down to a few burning coals, and the room was frigid. It was dark, and it took her a minute to find the light switch. When the lights wouldn't come on, she realized that there had been a power failure sometime during the night. She managed to get to the windows where she saw that the crashing sound had come from a slide of the roof due to falling snow on some metal rubbish barrels near the front entrance. It was still snowing, and the depth had reached well over two feet with high drifts banked against buildings and fences along the street.

The power was out everywhere. No lights were visible on the street or in any of the stores. She was surprised that the automatic generator had not kicked in as it usually did when the building lost power. She found her flashlight and hoped that the batteries still had enough charge left in them to shed some light into the room until daylight broke. There were a few wood logs still in the basket beside the stove, and she tossed them onto the burning coals, stoking the bed until some small shoots of flame began to wrap around the fresh wood. Still shivering, she stoked the fire once more, then took Silk by the collar, and headed toward the cellblock to check on Sean.

She pulled the dead bolts back on the heavy oak door leading to the cellblock and pushed it open. Silk was tugging to be free of her hold, but she pulled him in tightly to her side, stopping just inside the doorway. She stood completely still, not breathing. She was listening for some sound of any kind from Sean, but there was not a whisper of a breath or a rustle of movement coming from the cellblock. She felt as if she had walked into a void. Except for the dim glow from the flashlight, it was pitch-black and cold. The flashlight beam was starting to die out, and she could barely see as she inched forward along the narrow corridor toward Sean's cell.

There were three small windows along the cellblock walls, and she detected just a hint of gray dawn reflecting on the dirty windowpanes. Sean's cell was at the end of the block, and it was dark except for the hint of morning light coming through the narrow window. She released Silk, and he moved ahead of her, crouching as if he were stalking some invisible prey. His belly was low to the floor as he moved toward the last cell.

Carly called out.

"Sean, are you okay? We had a power failure."

No answer.

By the time she got to the cell door, Silk was already inside. The door was open, its lock tripped by the power outage, and the cell was empty. Carly felt a cold draft wrapping around her legs, and she knew that it was coming from the rear door to the cellblock. "Silk, come out of there. Come with me."

The dog was reluctant to leave the empty cell, but he obeyed Carly. She took him by the collar again and walked past Sean's cell to the rear of the block. Before she got there, she could see that the back door was wide open. Snow was blowing inside with each gust that skimmed across the open pastureland behind the building. She knew what had happened. The cell lock tripped when the power went out. The generator, if it had kicked in, would have refreshed the security of the lock. Sean had heard the lock trip and took advantage of the opportunity to escape. He had no shoes or clothing other than the jail jumpsuit and slippers, which he had put on earlier. Scott had taken the rest of his belongings and placed them in the locker in the front office.

"He just walked out into this weather in bare feet with nothing more on than that jumpsuit!" she said aloud.

She was frantic and pulled the door closed before she ran back along the corridor and out into the main room again to call Scott on her cell phone. He answered after a few rings.

"Scott, Sean Malone is gone."

"What are you talking about, Carly?" he said. "How can he be gone?"

"The power failure tripped the cell door latch, Scott, and I think he just walked out. The back door was wide open. Some falling snow woke me up, and when I realized the power had failed, I went right out back to check the cellblock. I knew the minute I opened the block door that something was wrong."

"I'll be right there, Carly, if I can get my car out of the driveway. If not, I'll walk. I'll be there. Call the state guys right now and get them up here. We're going to need a lot of backup on this."

He hung up, angry with himself for not getting that latch inspected when he should have.

Carly called the state police barracks in Burlington and requested help. The desk sergeant tried to be accommodating.

"We'll try to get someone up there right away, Officer Richardson. Can't guarantee how soon because the roads are not even plowed out here yet. If the weather breaks, we'll send a helicopter up with two men for air support. They might be able to get that there before the trucks with the dogs and snowmobiles anyway."

She thanked him and then made her way slowly back to the open cell, not quite sure what she was looking for but hoping to find something that might help.

Everything seemed to be in order. She had found one of the hurricane lamps in the front office and brought that with her to get more light. While she was searching the cell, her eyes fell upon a folded sheet of paper on top of the bed pillow. It looked like the notepaper that was kept in the cell desks. When she picked it up, she saw her name scrawled in pencil across the sheet. She brought it over to the desk and unfolded it. Sean had written her a note. It was scribbled and looked like it was written in haste.

> Couldn't face a court trial. Sorry for what I did to Kate and Maura. Sorry for what I did to you too. The bloody

snow just got to me. It just kept coming down freezing everything. My soul froze up with the rest of the world. Kate was leaving me and taking Maura, and I tried to stop her before she got out of the house, but she just kept running. I went crazy and headed the truck for them.

Carly cursed into the empty building.

"Sorry? You killed your whole family and my fiancé, and all you can say is *sorry*? You *are* a sorry wretch, and I'm going to hunt you down and bring you in if it's the last thing I do."

She ran back into the main office room, threw her heavy jacket and boots on, then grabbed her service revolver and handcuffs and pushed at the front door to free it from the snow that had blocked it. The storm had diminished to a few flurries, and there was enough morning light to give her at least some visibility beyond the building. She could hear the plows in the distance, but there was no sign of Scott. *He must be stuck*, she thought. *Can't wait for him.*

She opened the rear service door again to see if there were any tracks still visible, but the ones she had seen earlier were now totally covered by snow. The back of the jail edged up to an old stonewall that marked off some unused pastureland. Beyond the pasture lay thick pinewoods that ran the length of the main road and ended at the lake near the Malone place. Carly figured that Sean had headed out into the woods, an area he probably knew well. She wondered how far he could make it with no shoes or outerwear to protect him from the harsh weather. She stepped out of the building only to find herself almost waist deep in heavy snow. She gave up the idea of trying to track Sean by herself, knowing she wouldn't get very far on her own.

The power came back on just as she reentered the building, and she headed for the desk phone in the office to put another call into the state trooper barracks and check on their progress. The same sergeant she had spoken with earlier answered the call. The roads had been cleared there, and he promised backup within an hour.

"We're sending the helicopter as soon as the visibility improves a little. Best way to find anyone in the woods in these weather conditions. We'll bring a couple of snowmobiles along in the truck, and we have two bluetick hounds that we use for tracking that will join the team. We're sending four officers up for you instead of the two we talked about. We'll get him, Officer Richardson. He can't get far in this stuff."

Carly thanked him and sat at the bench by the front window, waiting for Scott.

The plows were moving along in tandem down Main Saint, and right behind them was Scott in his pickup truck. He pulled up in front of the building, and Carly ran outside to meet him.

"Are you okay, Carly? You look awful."

"Yeah? Well, it's been a rough morning so far. The troopers are sending some help from the Burlington barracks. We just have to sit it out until they get here. I am pretty sure Sean headed off into the woods, and there is no way we can get through there without some equipment. C'mon, let's get inside where it's warm."

The state police arrived within the hour. Four men, two dogs, three snowmobiles, and a helicopter beating the air above them in a steady cadence before it landed to the side of the building in an area cleared of snow. They all gathered in the main room of the building to get a briefing from Carly. It was around seven thirty in the morning, and Carly told them she thought he had been gone for about four hours.

"I was awakened around five thirty by a loud noise outside. Turned out it was just falling roof snow, but that was when I realized that the power was out. The cell lock circuit tripped, and he just got out and through the back door. There were some tracks earlier, but they're all covered over now."

"Do you think he knows those woods?" one of the troopers asked.

"Oh yeah," Carly replied. "I know he used to go hunting in there, and the woods end at the lake near an old abandoned sawmill, which is right below the Lakeview Farm main house. Our best bet is to use the snowmobiles to get through the woods and down to the lake," she told the lieutenant.

"Did he have any outer clothing on him?" he asked.

"No," Carly replied. "He was in an orange jail jumpsuit, no coat, no shoes that I know of. Don't know how he can last very long out there, dressed the way he is. Ought to be able to spot him pretty easily if he is still trying to push his way through. The woods stretch for about two or three miles before ending at the lake, so we can cover ground in pretty good time."

She showed them the note that Sean had left and then put it in her jacket pocket. The hounds were yapping to get moving, and Silk joined in on the noise. Carly decided to take him along, and she harnessed him up, keeping him close to her side. He knew Sean, so he could be useful in picking up his scent. Carly grabbed a piece of Sean's clothing and let the dogs sniff at it for a few minutes to get the scent. Scott locked the building, and they all headed out to begin the hunt.

THIRTY-EIGHT

The lieutenant and two of the troopers started up the snowmobiles, and loaded the dogs onto the sleds being towed by the snowmobiles. Scott, Silk, and Carly got in the helicopter with the other two troopers. They reviewed the search plan they had drawn up and then headed out. The snowmobiles moved across the back pasture toward the woods, sending up rooster tails of snow in their wakes. The helicopter lifted, hovering over the entrance to the wooded area like a hawk watching for the slightest rustle of prey on the ground below. There was not a track of man or animal in sight anywhere. The snow had accumulated an additional twenty-two inches since the day before, and five of those inches had fallen since the early hours of the morning. Carly nudged Scott to get his attention above the noise of the helicopter blades.

"This is going to be tough. Any mark that Sean might have left will be long gone by now," she said.

"Yeah, look at it down there! I don't even see animal tracks anywhere. I don't know how long he can survive out in this, dressed in that prison issue."

The helicopter made a sharp right turn and passed back over the snowmobiles below. Birds scattered everywhere, frightened by the noise coming at them from above and below.

Carly watched the snowmobiles as they skied across the flat ground toward the edge of the woods. When they reached the end of the pasture, they separated. The lieutenant moved to the right. One trooper moved left, and one headed straight into the heavily treed pine grove. The underbrush was thick and heavy with snow, and the trees were close to each other, making the going slow and treacherous.

The pilot found a large flat clearing about a quarter of a mile into the woods where the snow had been blown off to one side, allowing for safe landing in what snow was left. Bitter cold slapped the team in the face as they exited the helicopter with Silk. Carly felt the frost building on her eyebrows and lashes. The wind had died down, but there were vagrant gusts here and there, blowing the snow every which way and making visibility difficult. The pilot lifted the helicopter and went on ahead, then circled back, repeating the pattern again and again. The dogs were on high alert, and when they were unleashed, they dashed forward and then tracked back to the ground team. Silk was still harnessed, and he stayed reluctantly at Carly's side, wanting desperately to join the hunting pack.

They all made it to the lake after two hours of tracking through the woods. The thick growth of trees and low shrubs had kept the ground free of any significant depth of snow, making the travel less formidable than going through the pasture. The snowmobiles had enough depth to move along, and the ground team was using snowshoes to keep them from sinking in the snow. By the time everyone reached the lakeside, the helicopter had already landed. They all gathered around it to discuss the next steps and to grab some hot cocoa, which was packed in two large thermos jugs. No one had seen any sign of Sean Malone from the ground or the air. They needed to figure out another plan of attack.

"We should have the helicopter fly around the perimeter of the lake," Scott said. "The ground team, with the dogs and the snowmobiles can track back through the woods. We'll meet back at the police station, let's say, by noon time."

By noon, the ground team had covered the area, and the helicopter had circled the perimeter of the lake twice. There was not a trace of Sean anywhere. Carly knew he had either found a hiding place in the woods, or he had headed back toward Lakeview Farm. She half expected to find him fallen in the woods, either immobilized by the cold or dead. Scott and Carly got back in the helicopter, and the others started up the snowmobiles. The group had been out in the bitter cold for over five hours, and they were all beginning to suffer from hypothermia and hunger.

They headed back to the police station to warm up and get some hot food and coffee. Scott called in an order from the pub for pizzas, and Carly put on a huge pot of coffee while the troopers gathered on the chairs and sofa in the front office. The three dogs wasted no time in finding a warm spot in front of the woodstove.

"I don't know how he would survive out in this cold," the pilot said to the group. "He's barefoot, with nothing on but the prison jumpsuit. We're bundled in layers and we're still freezing."

"I know, it's pretty baffling," Scott replied.

"It's impossible for him to have made it very far. But we tracked all over the woods and didn't see hide nor hair of him. And that orange jumpsuit would have been visible unless he is holed up in some animal's den out there. The dogs would have picked up the scent someplace. I can't figure it. Not even a footprint."

"I know he is out there and not too far away," Carly said. "He's made it to the lake and found some shelter somewhere. I don't think he is in those woods, guys."

"I have to agree with you, Officer Richardson," the lieutenant said.

"He would be unable to move by now. The cold would have done him in. I suspect he has made it to the other side of the lake and he's holed up somewhere. It's getting too late to hunt for him any more today. I suggest we start first thing in the morning. But let's check out his house before we disband today. If he made it through the woods, he may have gone back there for clothing and shoes. We don't need the helicopter, so, Dave, you can head back to Burlington, but I do want the dogs and the rest of you to go to the farm to check it out." They finished the pizza, and Carly and Scott got into the department truck, telling the troopers to follow them out to Lakeview Farm.

The sun had started to set, and the sky had cleared, but the temperature had dropped to ten degrees, and the roads were starting to ice up, making the traveling hazardous as they got further away from the center of town. By the time they reached Lakeview Farm, it was nearly dark. The vacant house loomed like a dark shadow over the snow-covered grounds. They moved forward into the driveway as far as they could then walked the rest of the way to the rear entrance of the house. The dogs, including Silk, were running loose now, noses to the ground, sniffing every object and crevice as they followed the group. Several crows had lined up along the rail fence, watching them as they neared the house. Carly tried to shoo them away, but they hung on to the fence rail, fluttering their wings for balance.

"Foul things," she said to Scott. "They are always around this place. I hate those birds."

No one had been near the place for a couple of days, and the new snow cover should have been unmarked, but it wasn't. There were fresh footprints leading from the garage to the rear door of the house. Carly noticed that the garage door was slightly open, and tire tracks, although mostly covered by snow, led from the garage and crossed the ground, disappearing in the street. Sean had made it to the house, just as she suspected.

"Scott, look over here," she whispered. "He's been here. Look at the tracks." Scott stopped then motioned to the others to be silent and to gather the dogs in while at the same time, pointing to the trail of prints leading to the house. Knowing that Sean was armed, they all took their service revolvers from their holsters and cocked them to fire. They moved with caution to the back door.

The door was locked, but the glass panes were broken, and Carly reached through the hole to open the door from the inside. The troopers entered the kitchen first, pistols drawn. All the dogs were leashed and sat ready for a command. Scott and Carly followed the troopers into the dark kitchen. They stopped and waited in silence, trying to detect even the faintest sound or movement.

With her flashlight on high beam, Carly moved ahead of the troopers into the family room and toward the staircase that led to the second floor. She knew the layout of the house well and could guide them around quickly. She scanned the family room for any sign that Sean might have been there. As she turned toward the staircase, her attention was drawn to the gun cabinet on the wall near the windows. She remembered that Sean had kept three rifles in that cabinet, but only two of them were still there, and the glass door of the cabinet was open. She motioned for the others to halt.

"He's armed," she whispered. "One of the rifles is missing from that gun cabinet. C'mon, we're going upstairs." She started to climb the stairs, motioning for the others to follow her then stopped suddenly on the second rung. There were wet footprints in the dust of the stairs, marks made by bare feet, leading all the way up to the second floor. The air was thick with tension. Carly, Scott, and the lieutenant moved ahead on the staircase in single file. The other two troopers remained at the bottom of the stairs, ready with pistols and dogs if needed. The stairs creaked with each step they took, and the progress was slow. They got to the top landing and edged themselves along the wall, pistols ready, stopping before passing any of the closed bedroom doors.

"He's gone," Carly whispered. "He was here, but he's gone. I don't sense him in the house."

"Are you sure, Carly?"

"Pretty sure, but I want to check the master's bedroom anyway."

She motioned to Scott and the lieutenant to move behind her and cover her while she opened the door to the room. Her flashlight scanned the room until the beam landed on a wet pile of orange cloth in the center of the large braided rug.

Carly stopped.

"He's changed clothing and took off. No telling how long he has been gone. He could be headed anywhere. He's dressed for the weather now."

The lieutenant grabbed his two-way radio and made a call to the Burlington barracks.

"I want troopers stationed at every bus and train terminal between Burlington and the Canadian border and at every highway exit along the interstate. We have an escapee on the run, Sean Malone. Description details are on file. He's armed and considered dangerous. Do what is necessary to bring him in. Set up roadblocks on the local main roads and check all trucks trying to pass."

Confirmation on the requests came back immediately.

"We might as well head back to town," Scott said.

"We aren't going to find him tonight."

They walked single file down the stairs with the leashed dogs close beside and gathered in the kitchen. The troopers left first, insisting that they be called if anything turned up before morning. Carly and Scott, with Silk between them, headed out to their truck. The full moon, its face uncluttered at last from passing storm clouds, silvered the surrounding landscape.

"Looks like we may get some help from Mother Nature tomorrow. Sky's finally cleared," Scott said.

Carly looked up at the star-filled sky, hoping Scott was right.

"I'm going to find him, Scott, if it's the last thing I do. I don't care what the weather is. I'm going to find him."

Scott put his arm around her shoulder and gave one final glance back at the house before starting up and heading back to town. Four crows were still perched on the fence rail, watching the truck as it left the driveway. They pecked at each other, squawking in ugly rasping sounds, then left, one by one, their dark bodies silhouetted across the face of the full moon as they flew over the rooftops of the house and barn.

THIRTY-NINE

"Carly, I'm staying with you tonight. No argument, okay?"

"More than okay! I don't feel like being alone tonight," she replied.

Carly fed Silk and put the leftovers in the oven while Scott poured a glass of wine for each of them and turned on the TV. The evening news was still on, and there was a quick clip about the search effort for Sean Malone. His picture filled the screen with the numbers for both the Saint Basile Police Department and the Vermont State Police running across the bottom of the screen in a streaming ribbon of text.

"Hey, Carly. Check this out. Sean's mug shot is all over the news!"

Carly left the kitchen and joined Scott on the couch to watch the news report.

"He couldn't have gone too far in this weather, Scott. I have a feeling that he is somewhere near the Lakeview Farm property at least until the weather breaks. I want to get out there again first thing in the morning." Carly said.

"The staties said they would be here early. Don't you want to wait for them?" Scott asked.

"No. I think we should get out there by daybreak. He'll go on the run again early. I want to check around that old sawmill that sits down at the edge of the lake. There are some old buildings scattered about, and he could have made it down there if he left from the house."

"What about his truck? He's going to need transportation," Scott said.

Carly nodded in agreement.

"I bet he drove that truck down there. There's an old service road that leads from the main road down to the mill. He could've plowed his way down there, and we would never have even noticed. That little road is easy to miss because there's a lot of heavy growth on either side of it at the entrance."

"Don't forget that he's armed, Carly. Given his history, I don't think he would hesitate to fire if he's cornered. Are you sure you want to deal with that without the backup from the troopers?"

"I'm not crazy about the idea either, but if we don't get out there first thing, if he is there, we'll lose him, Scott!"

The oven timer went off, and she got up to get their dinner. She fixed two plates and brought them into the living room. Scott was stretched out on the sofa, sound asleep! They were both exhausted from the tension-filled day, and Carly decided not to wake him. She threw the afghan over him and turned off the TV.

"C'mon, Silk. Let him sleep."

The dog followed her into the kitchen and waited while she finished her dinner. It was nine thirty by the time she got into bed herself. Silk curled up at the foot of the bed, and Carly set her alarm clock for 5:00 a.m. She lay awake for a while, staring out her window. The night was still clear, but wisps of clouds were beginning to gather, hinting at a coming change. The weather forecast had called for a clear night with just a chance of light snow the following day. Carly fell asleep hoping that they got this one right.

She was awakened at 5:00 a.m. by the piercing ring of her alarm clock. Dawn was just starting to break, and the sky was streaked with clouds tinted crimson and orange by the rising sun. The snow glowed pink where the sun began to touch it, and she could hear the winter birds singing their welcome to the morning. A cardinal perched on the bedroom windowsill, pecking for scraps of berries from the shrubbery below. For a moment, she forgot about the difficult day she and Scott were facing and enjoyed the subtle movements of the dawn.

Scott was already up, and she could smell the fresh pot of coffee he had brewed.

"Come on, Carly. Get up! Breakfast is ready, and we need to get out of here," he called to her.

"I'll be right there. Just going to take a quick shower. Would you let Silk out for me?"

"Okay, but I'm giving you ten minutes, tops!" he called back.

Scott had scrambled up some eggs and was just buttering the toast when Carly walked into the kitchen.

"Good morning," she said, giving him a quick hug. "Are you still tired?"

"No," he replied sarcastically. "I had great sleep on the sofa last night! How come you didn't wake me?"

"You looked too peaceful, and I was exhausted myself. I figured we both needed all the sleep we could get."

They finished eating and packed up their gear. Carly checked her service revolver to make sure it was loaded before she put it into her holster. She put the leather harness on Silk because it was easier to control him if he got anxious and wanted to chase something. By the time they were in the truck and heading out, it was just past six o'clock. "Scott, I want to get down to that old sawmill as quickly as we can. Sean used to go down there once in a while, Kate said. I know there are some old buildings there, and he could be holed up in one of them until he thinks the coast is clear."

"Okay, but have *you* ever been down there?" Scott asked her.

"Just once, with Kate and Maura, in the fall. We went out for a walk, and Kate wanted to go down there and look around. It's nothing special. Just a lot of broken-down shed buildings and an old well that is right near the saw. Kate thought maybe they used the well water to cool the saw mechanisms down. It was covered over with some rotted planks, so we didn't actually see it open."

"Who owned the place, do you know?" Scott asked.

"Not sure, but I think it may have been the original owners of Lakeview Farm. Kate was pretty sure it was part of their deed," Carly replied.

Scott had been quiet for most of the ride out to Lakeview Farm. Carly finally asked him what was on his mind. Scott pulled the truck over to the side of the road.

"Carly, I'm still not clear on what the game plan is right now. If Sean is holed up at the mill, we need to have an action plan in place, don't you think? Also, did you let the state guys know we were coming up here this morning?"

"I told the lieutenant that we were going to check this place out. He said he would send a cruiser up here as soon as the morning shift came on, and I said I'd call him if we found anything before then. Those guys should be here around eight o'clock," she said.

"Okay, but how do you want to proceed when we get there? We can't just jump out of the truck and go running down the hill in a full charge!"

"You're right. We can park the truck at the road entrance. It's not a long walk down, and it's heavily treed, so the snow shouldn't be that hard to walk through. We can split up when we get at the end of the road and circle around the place then meet right at the lake edge. The buildings are pretty much open, so it shouldn't be too hard to see through them. And they're not spread far apart, so if one of us gets into trouble, the other can back up pretty fast."

"All right, but keep your two-way on emergency please," Scott told her. "We can just push the Alert button to flash if there's trouble."

He leaned over, and taking her chin in his hand, he turned her face to him.

"I don't want anything to happen to you, Carly. You be careful."

"I will, I promise," she said. "You do the same."

Scott moved the truck back out into the road, and within five minutes, they were at the access road to the sawmill. He pulled the truck into a small clearing at the roadside, and they got out, with Silk at a close heel to Carly, and moved toward the entrance of the access road. They hadn't noticed when they passed it to park, but the road had recently been plowed out.

Carly stopped, pointing at the tire tracks.

"He's been here, Scott," she said.

"Nobody plows this road out. He must have moved his truck down here. No wonder we couldn't find it!"

Scott walked a little way down the road, examining the tracks as he moved.

"I think he may still be down there, Carly. These tracks show a single path, not one that went back and forth. Call the troopers right now, and be sure to tell them we think we may have found Sean Malone, and they need to get here as quick as possible. I'll see if I can get Jim out here right away too. We're going to need all the help we can get," Scott said.

Carly got on her cell phone and called the barracks in Burlington, while Scott tried to reach Jim.

"The troopers are on their way," Carly said. "They should be here in about a half hour. I think we should go on down anyway. A lot can happen in thirty minutes."

"Are you sure you don't want to wait? I got Jim, but he's on a callout at Marlboro Road. Said he'd try to get here when he finished up," Scott said.

"I don't want to wait. Come on, we'll just go slow and real quiet. I'll keep Silk on the harness."

They started down the steep slope of the narrow road. Carly had been right about the snow. The trees had kept most of the snow out, and the road had been plowed enough to let them move easily. Their boots made loud crunching noises as they broke through the frozen crust. Silk kept close to Carly's side with his ears perked up and his nostrils quivering. He kept his head high and looked straight ahead at the clearing below.

By the time they got halfway down the road, they could see the lake ahead of them. It was frozen solid, and here and there, small wooden sheds perched on the ice, waiting for some Sunday fishermen to come and spend the day drinking beer and dropping fishing lines into holes in the frigid lake. Scott held his arm in front of Carly, stopping her.

"Look over there, behind those pine trees. There's something there."

Carly looked toward the direction of his point.

"Let's walk down a little farther," she suggested. "I see it but can't make out what it is."

They walked another twenty yards as quietly as they could.

"Scott, I think that's Sean's truck!" Carly said. "Can you make it out?"

Scott motioned for her to stay where she was as he moved forward along the tire tracks another ten yards. He turned and called back to her in a low voice.

"That's it, Carly. It's the truck, all right."

He moved back to her quickly.

"He must be still down there, but where is he holed up? Those sheds are all pretty open. We can see right through them."

"Yeah, but the saw shed isn't fully open. It's only open to the lake. He's got to be in there. Do you see any fresh footprints around?"

"Too far away to tell," he said. "Let's split here. You go to the right of the saw shed like we talked about, and I'll circle around to the left and get down to the lake."

Carly moved away to the right, getting out of the road and into the shelter of the trees. She could hear crows cawing above her, and when she looked up, she saw four or five of the large black birds slowly circling above the sawmill. The sight of the black birds triggered memories of her frequent encounters with them at Lakeview Farm. She felt the familiar chill creeping over her and pulled the collar of her jacket up tightly to her chin.

"Nasty birds," she muttered under her breath.

The crows circled overhead once more and landed, one by one, on the roof of the saw shed, watching her as they perched quietly on the far end of the beam.

She crouched down in the snow, watching for any movement around the shed. Silk lay down beside her, still alert, but now with his hackles raised. He started to growl in a low throaty sound.

"Be quiet, Silk. There's nothing there," Carly whispered to him.

She had no sooner spoken when she saw a shadow creep across the snow at the entrance to the saw shed. It slid into the shed from the side facing the lake. At the same time, she saw Scott moving at the other end of the shed. She wanted to warn him but didn't want him to move just yet. She was sure that Sean had just entered the saw shed and was afraid that he would see Scott. She cocked her revolver and inched forward, holding Silk as tightly as she could. He was straining at his harness, trying desperately to break loose. He had picked up a familiar scent and wanted to chase. Carly was able to keep a cover by staying off the access road, and she finally made her way through the side brush to the end of it. She was moving toward the entrance side of the shed when she spotted Scott coming around to the exit end. He saw her, and she motioned for him to stay where he was as she pointed to the area of the shed that held the saw. He stopped, raising his revolver in both hands in front of him.

FORTY

Carly's heart was pounding so hard that she thought it might burst through her chest. She tried to move closer to the shed while keeping Silk close at her side at the same time. He was wriggling and pulling, trying to free himself from the leather harness. A flash of movement in the shed caught her eye. Just as she edged closer to get a better view, Sean Malone stepped into a patch of sunlit ground near the front entrance of the shed. He was no more than thirty feet from her, but his back was to her, and his attention was focused on something near the lake.

Scott was well hidden, and although Sean looked in the direction of Scott's hiding place, he didn't seem to detect his presence. With the sun casting more light as it rose higher, Carly could see an area directly in front of Sean, near the saw, that looked like a pile of rotten old wooden planks strewn about the ground. She recognized this as the place where the abandoned well had been covered. Sean was walking toward the pile when Silk suddenly broke free from Carly's hold on the harness and rushed, snarling and barking toward Sean.

"Silk, no…stop!" she yelled.

Scott saw the dog getting ready to lunge, and he stepped forward out of the brush, aiming his revolver directly at Sean.

"Freeze!" he yelled. "You're surrounded, Sean. Drop the gun!"

Ignoring Scott, Sean spun around to face the growling dog, pointing the rifle at the dog's chest. In a split second, Silk made a leap at him, knocking him backward onto the rotten wooden planks. A shot flew from the rifle, wounding the dog, as he and Sean Malone fell together through the rotten wood into the ancient well below.

Both Carly and Scott rushed to the gaping hole in the ground. Carly was screaming.

"No, oh no, Silk! Scott, he shot Silk! He shot him!"

The dog was whimpering from the bottom of the well, but there were no sounds coming from Sean Malone.

"Silk is alive, Carly. Listen. He's making noise down there. We'll get him out. We'll get him," Scott said.

Scott turned on his service light and flashed the beam along the walls of the well and finally found the bottom. The circular walls were constructed with large blocks of stone, now covered with moss and slime from the lingering dampness. The well itself was about ten feet in diameter and at least twenty feet deep. Scott moved his light across the bottom, searching for both the dog and Sean. He could see large shards of rotten wood strewn about the floor, pieces of the planks that had broken when Sean fell against them. He suddenly turned to Carly.

"Carly, I see Silk. Look, he's lying down against the wall. He's breathing, Carly."

Carly knelt at the rim of the well calling softly to her wounded dog. Scott was kneeling beside her, and he moved the light slowly across the bottom of the well until it came to rest on the body of Sean Malone. Sean was on his back, and it looked like there was some blood on the side of his head. Scott couldn't tell if he was breathing.

"I have Sean in the beam, Carly. Look over here."

She took her eyes from Silk, and let them follow the flashlight beam.

"Is he dead?" she whispered.

"I don't know. I can't tell if he's breathing or not. Looks like his right leg is broken. He may be unconscious from the fall. Do you see the rifle anywhere up here?"

"No, it's not here," she said as she looked around the gaping hole. "It must have fallen with him."

"Have to get down there, Carly," Scott said. "At the very least, I want to try to get Silk out of there. The troopers can help with Sean when they get here. There's an old wooden ladder leaning up against the wall near the windows. It might be long enough to reach to the bottom."

"Scott, that ladder looks like it's falling apart. You should let me go. I'm smaller and lighter. That ladder is in bad shape and might not be able to handle much weight. You can hold it from here while I climb down. Then we can use that length of rope over there to make a sling for Silk. I can cradle him in my jacket and harness him with the rope so you can pull him up. I'll stay right behind on the ladder."

"I don't know, Carly. We don't know for sure if Sean is knocked out or dead down there. What are you going to do if he wakes up all of a sudden?"

"Scott, Silk is my dog. I have to get him out of there, and that ladder will never hold your weight. Now just shut up and let's get this done, okay?"

He leaned back on his heels, throwing his arms up in exasperation, but knowing at the same time that she was going down there with or without his help. He got up and walked to the shed wall to get the ladder and the rope. The ladder looked as if it would extend to twenty feet, and the rope was about ten feet longer, but in poor condition. It had been lying on the ground for a long time and was showing signs of rot in several spots. He worried that it would break apart while he was trying to haul the dog up to the surface.

"Carly, I don't like the looks of this rope. It's in pretty bad condition, and I'm not sure it will hold Silk without breaking apart."

She gave the rope a quick look, noticing the frayed spots on it.

"It has to work, Scott. It's all we have right now. We'll just take it slow." Scott was hoping that the troopers would show up and help them out, but when he checked his watch, he figured they were still a good half hour away.

They anchored the rope around two of the steel legs on the old saw and then lowered the ladder into the dark hole until they heard the loud thump that signaled a landing on the well floor. Carly took off her jacket and tied it to the rope. She would fashion a litter for Silk when she reached the bottom of the well.

"Ready?" he asked.

"I'm ready. Just let me climb over the rim and get a foothold on a rung. I'll get down a couple of feet, then you can start to lower the rope," she said.

"Carly, try to step on the sides of the rungs instead of the middle. If the ladder is rotted, then the center of those rungs will be rotted and won't hold you."

"I'll be careful. Just give me a hand here," she replied. She took the high-intensity headlamp out of her jacket pocket and adjusted it on her forehead, keeping her hands free to maneuver her descent.

Scott helped her over the rim and onto the first rung of the ladder and then lowered the rope and jacket.

The ladder creaked under Carly's weight, and she stayed still for a moment to get her balance. The well walls were damp and slimy with green algae. Spiders and centipedes of all sizes crawled over the stones in every direction, and the odor rising from the bottom reminded her of the smell that she had encountered in the barn at Lakeview Farm. It smelled like death. She gritted her teeth and started her slow descent, stepping carefully on the round rungs of the old ladder. Her vision was limited with the only light coming from the small lamp strapped to her head. She could still hear Silk, whimpering quietly, but she could not detect any sound at all coming from Sean Malone.

Her descent was slow because of the instability of the old ladder, and as she moved further down, a few of the rungs cracked under her weight. She kept her attention on reaching the bottom and not on her fear that she might not make it back up.

Scott called to her from the rim of the well.

"Carly, are you okay? This ladder doesn't feel as if it will hold out."

"I'm almost at the bottom, Scott. Two more rungs."

"Are you keeping your feet to the sides and not the center of the rungs?" he called.

"Yes, Scott. I'm trying to. Just please be quiet. You're making me nervous."

She stepped down and felt the damp ground beneath her feet. It was soft and slippery with moss. She took her flashlight from her belt and directed the beam to where Silk was lying. He raised his head as she approached him, weakly wagging his tail.

"It's okay, boy. You're going to be okay. We are going to get you out of here," she told him.

She could see Sean's body lying about four feet away from the dog, and she walked over to him and knelt down, keeping a safe distance. He was breathing, but he appeared to be unconscious. She looked around him for the rifle but didn't see it near his body. His right leg looked as if it was broken, and there was blood under his head and right shoulder. She nudged his side with her foot, but there was no response. She called up to Scott.

"Scott, Sean is breathing. He's knocked out, and his leg looks broken. Seems to be a head injury, too. I'm going to get Silk wrapped up in my jacket and then truss him with the rope. I'll let you know when I have him secure."

Carly went back to Silk and laid her jacket on the ground beside him. The bullet had grazed his shoulder, but it hadn't penetrated the skin. There was some bleeding at the wound site, but it wasn't heavy enough that Carly wanted to abort the plan to lift him out. She kept talking softly to the dog as she eased him over to her jacket and lifted his body to place him in the center of it. Then she ran the rope through the sleeves and under the jacket so that she could fashion a sling. Silk was still whimpering with pain, but he let her get him into the makeshift litter. She looped the rope around the dog's hind end and front end and then called up to Scott.

"Scott, I have him secured. You can start lifting him. I'll be right beside him on the ladder."

Scott started to pull on the rope, slowly lifting the dog from the ground. Carly grabbed the rope to help guide it and then stepped back on the ladder to start her climb. She was about to step on the third rung when she felt a viselike grip on her right ankle. She was yanked from the ladder and violently dragged back onto the damp well floor, somehow managing to land on her feet. She was able to twist herself around and found herself facing Sean Malone. He was stretched out on the well floor with both hands around her left ankle in a deathlike grip. She raised her right leg and delivered a hard kick to his head, causing him to release her ankle and roll over in pain. She released her revolver from its holster and cocked it, readying it to fire. Before she had a chance to aim, Sean had rolled back on his stomach, grabbing both her ankles and pulling her to the ground with him. Her gun fell from her hand and landed a few feet away from Sean. In an instant he was on her, with his hands at her throat.

"If you make one sound, Carly, I'll kill you. Understand?"

She nodded her head. Still keeping pressure on her throat, he turned his head to locate where her gun had fallen, and when he spotted it, he moved his good leg near it to try and get it closer to him. Carly took advantage of his split-second inattention and thrust her knee hard into his groin.

He rolled off her, yelling in pain.

"You're dead," he groaned.

Carly jumped up and grabbed her gun. As she did, she spotted the rifle lying about three feet away from Sean. He saw her move toward it and rolled himself over so that it was within arm's reach. Before Carly could kick it away and get her own gun aimed, Sean had the rifle in his hands, aiming it at her chest. Scott, thinking that Carly was moving toward the surface, had been concentrating on getting Silk to the top of the well and didn't hear the commotion below until the dog was nearly at the rim. He pulled at the rope hard and got the dog over the edge and safely onto the ground beside him, and then he realized that Carly was still at the bottom of the well.

"Carly, are you all right? What's going on? Carly, answer me. Are you all right?"

His flashlight scanned back and forth across the well floor until he saw Sean lying on the ground with the rifle aimed at Carly, and Carly standing over him with her own gun drawn and aimed at Sean's head. Scott knew that he didn't have time to get to the bottom, so he grabbed his own revolver, cocked it, and using the flashlight, aimed it directly at Sean.

"Sean, drop the weapon. Now. I'm aimed at you, and so is Carly. You don't have a chance. Drop it, Sean, or I will shoot to kill." There was silence, then a scuffling noise, then the sharp crack of a single shot shattered the cold morning air. Its echo rippled in waves against the damp stone walls of the well before it trailed off into a dreadful silence.

EPILOGUE

"I wish you wouldn't do this, Carly," Scott said.

She continued packing, trying not to look at him as she worked.

"Scott, my mind is made up. I have to get away from all this snow before it changes me the way it changed Sean. I can't finish this winter out, and I can't take another one here. I figure if I get far enough away, I'll be all right again."

"Where will you go?" he asked. "Why won't you tell me where you are going?"

"Because I don't know for sure myself, Scott. I'm heading South, and that's all I know for now. Someplace hot and steamy. Someplace as far away from snow as I can get."

"So it doesn't matter to you that I'm here and that I love you?"

"It does matter, Scott, it matters more than you can imagine, but I can't love you here. Don't you understand? I can't love you back if I stay here. Every time it snows, I'll see Rob dying on a roadside or Kate's broken body buried in a snowdrift or Maura's dead blue eyes staring up at me from that hole. I can't do it anymore. And it's not fair to you."

She pulled another suitcase from the bedroom closet and packed the few remaining pieces of clothing in it. Scott knew that he was not going to change her mind.

"Will you at least let me know where you end up?" he asked.

She locked the suitcase and turned to face him. This was the moment of truth for both of them. "Scott, I don't want you to be hurt. I care a lot about you. I love you. But I'm not ready for the kind of commitment that I think you want from me. I need some time alone. So no, I probably won't let you know where I am right away, at least not until I get myself sorted out. I'm so sorry, but I won't be any good to you or anyone else until I am *good* to myself. Can you understand that?"

She turned away from him so he wouldn't see her cry. The look on his face told her that she had broken his heart. She grabbed the two suitcases and headed for the living room.

"At least let me help you with those," he said.

She put the bags down, and he grabbed them and took them outside to her car. She picked up the two envelopes on the counter, one addressed to her parents and the other to Rachel, and walked outside to her mailbox, raising the flag to let the mailman know she had a pickup in the box. Scott walked beside her back to the front door. Silk was waiting inside, pressing his nose against the glass as he watched them. Scott took Carly in his arms and held her tightly to him. She wanted to kiss him, but she pushed him back instead.

"Scott, I have to get going before I get caught in this storm. You take care of yourself," she said, leaving him at the bottom of her front stairs.

"When I'm ready, I'll let you know where I ended up. I promise I will do that," she said.

"Carly, I'll join you anywhere. You know that. All you need to do is ask me."

She put the leash on Silk and locked the front door, leaving the key on the counter for the landlord. The storm clouds were starting to gather, and she hoped she would make it through New York before it hit. Before she started the car up, she pulled out the road map and looked at the line she had drawn with the pink highlighter marker that traced the route from Vermont to Vermilion Bay, Louisiana, a place where there would be absolutely no chance of snow.